PENGUIN METRO READS
KISS AND TELL

Nistula Hebbar is senior assistant editor at the *Financial Express* in New Delhi and reports politics for a living. She was born and educated in Delhi, and has been a journalist for the last eleven years. She has covered everything from the state of the city's drains to the offices housing its high and mighty.

Addicted to pulp fiction, she firmly believes in its magical healing powers.

Kiss & Tell

Nistula Hebbar

Penguin
metro reads

An imprint of Penguin Random House

PENGUIN METRO READS

USA | Canada | UK | Ireland | Australia
New Zealand | India | South Africa | China | Singapore

Penguin Metro Reads is part of the Penguin Random House group of companies
whose addresses can be found at global.penguinrandomhouse.com

Published by Penguin Random House India Pvt. Ltd
4th Floor, Capital Tower 1, MG Road,
Gurugram 122 002, Haryana, India

First published in Penguin Metro Reads by Penguin Books India 2012

ISBN 9780143416241

Typeset in Bembo Roman by SŪRYA, New Delhi
Printed at Repro India Limited

www.penguinbooksindia.com

This is a legitimate digitally printed version of the book and therefore might not
have certain extra finishing on the cover.

For my mother, Kumuda Hebbar.
You are missed every day.

Prologue

Janaki hated red-eye flights. The early morning rush to get dressed and the sickly feeling she got stealing out of a city at dawn. But her office had booked her on the earliest possible flight to Chennai, and there was no helping it. Janaki had been rushed the previous evening with some last minute political developments, and hadn't looked too closely at her ticket. 'The sadists at the travel desk probably thought this was a good joke,' she said angrily to herself, vowing to get even when she got back. 'Just wait for the next one who wants to get a bloody passport done in a jiffy,' she added viciously. As a reporter, Janaki often felt she was a passport officer herself, having to help out so many colleagues.

Putting it out of her mind, Janaki's thoughts returned to her current assignment. Travelling to Tamil Nadu to cover the assembly elections just fell into her lap after her colleague and bête noire Shakira Banerjee had fallen ill. Janaki leapt at the chance; lately, being away from Delhi seemed like an escape.

As she applied her regulation kajal in her brandy-coloured eyes, Janaki shied away from examining too closely just why that was so. She knew, in her heart of hearts, that her boyfriend Saurabh, the only man she had ever seriously been with since college, was the cause of her uneasiness.

As a political correspondent for the *Indian Mail*, a serious newspaper—one of the big three in Delhi—Janaki was doing fairly well. She was twenty-eight, attractive in an earthy, voluptuous way, and had a steady boyfriend who she planned to marry when the time was right. It was only that last bit that was giving her the jitters. It seemed that Saurabh, an independent documentary-maker mostly of sponsored government work, was quite happy to only take on sporadic work and spend the rest of his days in a haze of pot smoke.

While Saurabh's long-haired, lazy persona had seemed attractive in 'rebel without a cause' college days, Janaki, who had been brought up with a strict work ethic by her university professor parents, was losing her patience with him. A yelling match with Saurabh the previous evening, when she found out that he had borrowed money from their college friends yet again, had not helped to improve her mood.

'Damn and blast,' she muttered to herself as she found that her favourite all-weather sandals had broken. 'Now I'm stuck with new shoes to break in, on top of everything else!'

Janaki's friends couldn't quite figure out why she persisted with Saurabh; after yesterday, even Janaki was beginning to wonder. She did a quick check of her toiletries bag—despite being a reporter of some experience, she hadn't quite managed to learn to travel light. 'So what, I'm high maintenance,' she always said to anyone who raised an eyebrow at her luggage. She refused to move out of her house without all her haircare and other products, at least two pairs of shoes and three changes of clothes. 'With the heat in Tamil Nadu being the way it is, I better have several changes of clothing,' was how she justified her hefty suitcase this time.

The intercom phone in Janaki's flat in east Delhi buzzed, signalling that her cab to the airport had arrived. It was still dark as she made her way downstairs from her third-floor flat. She greeted the cabbie, who was familiar to her since she had lived in the area for three years now, and had used that service quite frequently.

The driver's name was Hoshiar Singh, a philosophical Jat from Rohtak, who regaled Janaki with political gossip from Delhi's neighbouring state and effectively prevented her from brooding on the long drive to the airport. As a journalist, it was expected of her to be interested in everyone's opinion of the state of the zeitgeist.

Unaware of the many admiring glances she got while waiting in line to check in, Janaki resolved that something had to give as far as she and Saurabh were concerned. 'What you want when you're eighteen and what you want when you're twenty-eight are different things,' her friend Kajal had often told her.

Janaki just couldn't bring herself to broach the topic with Saurabh, however. He always dismissed her issues as a joke and ended up making her laugh at his antics. In a strange way, the dynamics in their relationship had changed from the equal one of classmates to an unequal one where Janaki took responsibility and Saurabh played the carefree youth.

Asking for an aisle seat, Janaki completed her check-in formalities, and she went in search of a bookstore. She needed to pick up the latest bio of one of the top contenders for the chief minister's chair in Tamil Nadu. 'I'll do all my thinking when I land,' she said resolutely to herself. Like Scarlett O'Hara, she needed no encouragement to postpone a decision.

One

'Hello?' Janaki said to the voice at the other end of the phone. 'Am I speaking to Mr Vishnu Singh? I'm Janaki Rao, from *Indian Mail*. I believe my colleague Deepak Sharma called you about me; I've just landed in Chennai and wanted to see you,' she said.

A deep voice at the other end replied very tiredly, 'Oh yes, Ms Rao, he did. What can I do for you?'

Well, thanks for the enthusiastic greeting, Janaki thought to herself as she negotiated her strolley up a particularly challenging set of stairs outside the Chennai office of her paper. Having arrived in the middle of the *agneenakshatram*, the star of fire period, of the southern summer (a particularly sadistic time to conduct assembly elections, she thought), she was rapidly melting into a pool of sweat, and wanted nothing more than to check into an air-conditioned room. That, alas, was not an option available to her, not with her having to leave for Madurai on the early morning bus tomorrow. Janaki thought longingly of her new air conditioner in her Delhi home, bought with that year's bonus.

Strictly speaking, the regional third front parties, especially the allies of the present government, were not Janaki's beat. The assignment belonged to the bombshell of their political team, Shakira Banerjee, or 'Banerjee of the shapely behind' as Janaki had dubbed her. A sudden outbreak of typhoid had laid Shakira low, and Simran Kher, their boss, had asked Janaki to pitch in at the last moment. 'Read up—Google is god in these cases—and carry a list of phone numbers. Who is asking you to reinvent the wheel?' she had said. Simran believed in the tough love school of reporter training. It was left to Deepak Sharma, the crack investigating guy on their team, to pitch in with some numbers, Vishnu Singh's among them.

Balancing the phone between her ear and shoulder, Janaki said, 'Mr Singh, I was hoping to get a background briefing on some of the politics of the state. I'm leaving for Madurai early tomorrow morning, so I can come to your office near Nungambakkam now, but I'm at T. Nagar, and it will take me a little time to get there with my suitcase,' she said.

She heard a barely concealed sigh and then a very resigned, 'Very well, please tell me where your office is; I will get you picked up.' Heaving a sigh of relief Janaki sank on to the steps to wait for the car. Despite the complaints she felt excited about the elections, which in this southern state were always very colourful and brimming with good stories. She tried to feel a little sympathy for Shakira, but just could not muster any.

Janaki had also never visited Chennai before, so it was a great chance to explore the city a little before she left. I will leave some time for it towards the end, she thought. She still had a list from her friend Narayani, who had demanded an impossible number of *thokkus* or pickles from the city's famous Grand Sweets shop.

~

Vishnu Singh, the fast-track blue-eyed bureaucrat of the present dispensation, put his phone down. 'Muthuswamy,' he said to his peon, 'tell Shivalinga, my driver, to go to this address in T. Nagar and pick up this journalist, Ms Janaki Rao.'

Vishnu had met Deepak Sharma during one of his rare stints in Delhi as a bureaucrat. Sharma was a good journalist and very discreet. I wonder what this girl wants, probably does not know the language and wants a quick-fix interpretation of the situation,

Vishnu thought. Deepak had called him yesterday, and, while he was tempted to say no, he knew he owed Deepak a favour.

'She's smart as a whip; you won't have to hold her hand on anything, just help her out with logistics and point her to some English-speaking guys in the districts to help her out,' Deepak had said to Vishnu. Well, I hope that's all there is, he thought. He vividly recalled Deepak's other colleague, Shakira Banerjee of the divine backside, who thought she only needed that appendage to get anything. When Shakira turned up at North Block it was an event worth heralding, with every officer and clerk following her progress with their tongues hanging out and drool spilling out like waterfalls. Vishnu had given her short shrift when he realized that her brains were not her best asset, and they leaked the moment she opened her mouth.

As he settled down to do his files, Vishnu glanced up at his mother's photograph on his desk. Lately, every time he called her up, all their conversation had been on how he needed to get married and settled and reproduce. Good thing Lucknow is so far away from Chennai, he thought to himself. Frankly, it gave him a headache. As a bureaucrat dealing with the finance and, for a while, the rural development department, he met new people every day, just nobody who grabbed his attention in any way. He was romantic enough to believe that attraction was necessary for him to commit. His relationships in college in Delhi had been the usual run till he had met Gayatri at the IAS academy. With beautiful hair, flashing eyes and long legs to wrap around himself, she got to him like no one else. Unfortunately, although amenable to an affair, she was determined to marry within her own community, and losing her remained a nagging ache within him. No woman he met since then had lived up to his memory of her.

Not that there had been a lack of women; it was amazing how many women were prepared to throw themselves at you just because you were in god's own service, the civil service of the country. Tall, slim and handsome, Vishnu knew he was considered a catch, but he was under no illusions over why. Ultimately it was the crassness of the social climbing which he saw in his professional life that got to him. He only had to meet a beautiful woman—and there were a huge number in Chennai—to begin wondering just what she was after. Not the best strategy to land a wife, he thought.

At thirty-six, Vishnu was a bachelor, and had a lukewarm 'friends with benefits' arrangement with his colleague Shashwati, posted in the boondocks in Andhra Pradesh, but the sex was getting so desultory that he wondered whether the monthly trips to Hyderabad were worth it. Being single in the hinterland of India was getting to Shashwati, turning her bitter, he thought. He had been attracted by her looks, reminiscent of Gayatri in that glacial way, and the fact that they had all been part of the same gang. At thirty-six, he was in no hurry, but his mother's endless nagging and the pervasive feeling of ennui was making him dissatisfied. After the elections, a holiday is in order, he thought.

A tentative knock intruded into Vishnu's thoughts. His room, kept at a temperature near freezing to beat off the hot Chennai summer, was humming with air conditioning. As he watched Janaki Rao walk towards him and extend her visiting card to him with a beautifully crooked grin, he felt an undeniable kick in his gut—something he hadn't felt in some time—a visceral sexual jolt at the sight of this petite yet curvy woman.

'Hi,' she said. 'Here is my card, sir; I'm Janaki Rao. I'm so glad you could send the car; the heat is amazing and, with the suitcase, I would have really struggled to find this place. Is it okay to leave the suitcase in the car?' she asked.

Stop this, Vishnu; she is Deepak's colleague; he'll kick your ass if you try anything, he cautioned himself. 'Hi! Oh yes, it's fine. I'll drop you at your hotel on my way home; please don't worry,' he said, extending his hand and gripping Janaki's surprisingly tough yet tiny hand in his. Physically she was not at all his type, as different from the glacial Gayatri as, well, volcanos and glaciers. As he watched a small trickle of sweat make its way into her kurta and between her ample breasts, he wished to god he was that trickle of sweat and not the puddle of sexual desire he was turning into.

Almost as if she could read his dirty thought, she looked straight up and into his eyes, laser sharp, and held his gaze with a directness that went straight to his balls. Those eyes could devour a man, he thought.

'Aren't you a little too young to be a political correspondent?' he asked, almost cringing at the patronizing tone that had somehow slipped out of his mouth.

A frown creased her forehead, but she quickly recovered. 'I'll take that as a compliment,' she said and smiled.

Well, well, well, Janaki thought to herself. Mr Singh is not too bad, probably married to one of those IAS begums. Tall, dark and undeniably handsome, although tall men had never been her type, as she stood at a petite five foot two. Saurabh was not really very tall. Suddenly Janaki wished that she had taken the time to wash up at the airport or at her Chennai office, her sweat-beaded face compared to an icy cool begum flashed before her eyes. My kajal must have run, I must look like a raccoon, she thought to herself. She was vain enough to want to impress this very impressive piece of manhood. A little preppier than I'd normally like, but whatever he has is working, she thought.

'Mr Singh, I know you are very busy, and I'll try not to take too much of your time. I really wanted to know about the self-help groups in Madurai, and some of the labour issues in the industrial belt that surrounds it,' she said, fishing out her notebook and pen. 'If you could also give me the numbers of some activists and rural development NGOs with whom the government liaises, it will be a help,' she said trying to sound all professional.

Vishnu rubbed his hand over his face and looked at this young woman: a little dishevelled, but undeniably hot. That blemish-free, light, coffee skin alone could be worth hours of foreplay. I'd start with the neck, he thought. He was a little taken aback at his reaction to this brandy-eyed, oomphy creature; Gayatri had been tall, fair and patrician in the extreme. Giving himself a mental shake, he replied, 'Yes, well, I have some numbers, but the thing to also realize is that the state government has been extremely persistent in requiring the rural banks to extend credit. The biggest problem facing self-help groups is that, despite good credit records within their groups, the banks don't trust women members. This despite the subsidy extended by the government to the banks to do just that.' His thoughts went to her even as he spoke. 'You must be feeling parched,' he said suddenly. 'Selvam!' he called his peon, 'Please get some tender coconut water for madam, and some for me too.'

Vishnu turned his attention back to Janaki. 'When did you start working for the *Mail*?' he asked. 'I don't recall meeting you when I was in North Block.'

'That's because I cover the National Resurgence Party, so I'm at party offices, not government ones,' she said naming the principal opposition right-wing party in the country. 'I don't go to North Block much,' she added. Oh no, you don't, Vishnu thought, otherwise I would surely have noticed.

Vishnu stared at her narrow wrist, light gold bangles gleaming against her skin, and wondered what she would look like in just the bangles, and maybe some chunky anklets. Stop this, your mother is right, there is a very thin line between being an eligible bachelor and a dirty old man, he said to himself. 'How long have you been working?' he asked instead, as they both waited for the coconut water.

'Well, around five years. Before this I was at the *Standard*, in city reporting, after which I got this job as a political correspondent,' she said. Fortunately for Vishnu, Selvam entered the room just then, carrying a tray with some coconut water and some roasted cashews.

As was her habit, Janaki flashed a grateful smile at Selvam, and thanked him. The poor man just blinked at the sight, and bent that much more deferentially towards her. Poor sod, though Vishnu, that smile can stop you in your tracks. 'Put it here and tell Mani to hold my calls,' he said. He fished around on his phone and began rattling off phone numbers to Janaki. 'This guy here has worked for six years on the dairy project of this self-help group; it is one of the more successful projects. He'll also help you get in touch with some of the others in the area,' he said.

Janaki dutifully wrote out all the numbers he gave her; she wanted to do a story on the rural resurgence and its effect on the politics. 'Could you also help me get actor Shashikanth's assistant's number? I want to do an interview when I'm in Madurai,' she said. Shashikanth was the new actor-politician on the firmament, and this was an important assignment. Vishnu scrolled back on his phone and gave her the numbers.

'Which hotel are you staying in?' he asked.

'Chennai Plaza, my office booked it. Is it on your way?'

'Yeah yeah, I'll drop you; no problem. Just give me a few minutes.'

Walking towards the car, Janaki surreptitiously did what her girlfriends called the 'slant-eyed checkout'. Head, torso, butt, legs. Checks out, she thought. Those endless legs to give you chase, hmm . . . As a short person she had a very envious appreciation of tall people and long legs.

A white Ambassador arrived at the portico of the ministry building. Vishnu opened the door for Janaki, keeping his fingers crossed that his chivalrous gesture, only designed to check out her butt, would not be taken as an affront to feminism.

'Thank you,' she said and slid over to the other side. Nice round thing, Vishnu thought as he gazed at her butt. Suddenly he realized that Janaki was regarding him steadily with those laser eyes of hers. Hurriedly he got into the car. They spent the journey to her hotel chatting about their various mutual acquaintances. Vishnu hoped and prayed that Janaki would forgive him his appraisal of her body.

'Um . . . where did you study exactly?' he asked her.

'Delhi University, both bachelor's and master's.'

'Me too; of course much before your time.'

Janaki smiled. She could sense that he was completely uncomfortable at having been caught eyeing the goods. She felt kind of sorry for him too. 'You must look me up when you get to Delhi,' she said.

'Of course,' he replied. 'And look, I'm sorry about the thing earlier,' he said awkwardly.

She laughed out loud. 'Maybe I'll make you pay for drinks then, when we meet in Delhi. I'd like to hold this over your head for some time; let's see what I can get out of it,' she said as the car reached her hotel.

Vishnu felt immeasurable relief. He also felt the surprise of knowing that she was really cool. 'A collegiate term, but appropriate I think,' he said to himself.

Two

'A very handsome man checked out my butt today!' Janaki declared to her college friend Srividya. Sri, as Janaki liked to call her, had come to her hotel and they were unwinding with a tall, cool glass of beer.

Sri's eyebrows went up in surprise. 'Who?' she asked. 'Are there any handsome men here?'

'Vishnu Singh,' said Janaki with a twinkle in her eye. When Sri looked at her doubtfully, she responded, 'He's not like that, really.' Then, as if in defiance of her friend's expression, she said, raising her glass in a toast, 'His own butt is not too bad either. I hope his wife truly appreciates it!'

'Oh, he's not married. He's probably not even seeing anyone.'

Janaki stopped midway through raising her glass.

'Is that even possible? Is there truly a single man out there who is eligible, straight, holds down a good job and wants to check out my butt?' she said as they collapsed in giggles.

Sri responded in kind, now fully into the girly conversation, 'Arrey, your butt is checkoutable, trust me. And, if you gave him one of your looks, bechara would not dare do anything!' In college Janaki was known to shred unwelcome suitors with a just a look, something Sri had not forgotten.

'Well, it was nice, you know. I have been with Saurabh since second year college, and sometimes I feel he has stopped seeing me. Sometimes even I forget what my butt looks like,' Janaki said

12

ruefully. 'Not to mention every day spent with heartland politicians, trying to be as demure as possible around them, for heaven forbid they get the wrong idea about you!' Escapes like this one, with her college friends, obligingly spread across the country, went a long way in reminding her of the effervescent person she had once been.

As they ordered room service and caught up on each other's lives, Janaki thought it might be nice to come home to Vishnu Singh. Well, even if he did check out my butt, that event is going to stay in Chennai; I'm leaving in a week, she told herself firmly.

Meanwhile, the subject of her thoughts stared moodily at a tall glass of beer, looking at children splashing in the pool of the Madras Gymkhana Club. Shipping talk flowed all around him, the Gym being a haunt of merchant shipmen and bureaucrats. Shit, he chastised himself, you're so bloody useless, man, you couldn't even check out her butt without coming off as a lecher! That girl showed more grace and sophistication than you did. He was still trying to figure out what had happened that afternoon.

Vishnu was generally known to be a smooth operator: 'This man can get a woman to remove her panties in record time and convince her that it was her idea the whole time,' is what his friend Ranbir Khanna used to say about him. Yeah right, Mr Smooth, Selvam would probably have been smoother, he thought. She had to bail me out. You are the take-charge guy, you should have been the cool one, he said to himself.

'Well, well, just what has put that frown on your face young man, Muthuswamy again?' S. Venkataraman, the finance Secretary of the state and his own mentor and guide, broke into Vishnu's reverie.

Vishnu stood up quickly and offered the old man a chair. Venkataraman had spotted Vishnu as a young probationer, brought him into the economic ministry and put him through his paces rigorously. He owed a lot of his present success to the man.

'Nothing sir, the weather is just a tad too heavy,' he said.

Venkataraman looked at Vishnu. Refusing the chair, but putting his hand on the young man's shoulder, he said, 'Perhaps you need a change of weather, son. In any case, you seem to be stuck here until the elections are over. Come to me then; we need to talk.' Then he slowly walked away.

Vishnu knew that he was a man of a few words, so if he said something, it probably held a lot of significance. He stayed standing until Venkataraman was far away, absorbed in his own thoughts. Now, what can that mean? Whatever, you'll probably handle that better than the woman. He quickly ordered his dinner. The thought of dining alone in his palatial home was not something he looked forward to.

Three

As the bus rattled on the road to Madurai, Janaki cursed her paper's travel office in Chennai for booking her on a video coach. Loud Tamil dialogue from the video playing and even louder music was giving her pounding headache. She put on her iPod and tried to block out everything and grab some shut-eye. After a couple of stops for refreshments, the bus reached Madurai in the evening, and Janaki got off and checked into a local hotel. She called some local stringers in Madurai, whose numbers she had taken from Sri.

The next morning dawned very bright, as was the case with southern summer mornings. People had warned her that a siesta was a must if she wanted to avoid heatstroke. 'But how do these politicians campaign in the heat?' she had asked Simran, the tough political editor and bureau chief at the *Mail*.

'Arrey, they will become MLAs and chief ministers and then earn a lot of money out of it. You won't become the editor by risking your health reporting them,' Simran had said laconically. 'You are in print media not television, *gadha mazdoori mat karo, ghoda mazdoori karo*,' she advised smiling.

In her early forties, Simran had covered umpteen elections and the whole gamut of political parties, leaving her with a very practical approach to reporting.

For Tamil Nadu, Janaki had worked out a peculiar schedule. She would start early and come back to the hotel by 11 a.m. and then only venture out after 4.30 in the evening. 'Except, I want you to catch a couple of rallies by Shashikanth, I believe he is attracting enormous crowds and he does a routine with his filmi dialogues,' Simran had told her.

Two days after arriving in Madurai, Janaki would get to see one such rally. Murugan, the local stringer for the Delhi-based *Daily News*, which didn't have a Madurai edition, was also going to be there to help with translation. Janaki had set up an interview with Shashikanth after the rally was over.

As was usual in a political rally, local artistes and party workers with some talent were keeping the crowd engaged before the star attraction turned up. Covering her head with a dupatta to keep the worst of the sun off her face, Janaki scanned the crowd and chatted about the elections with local journalists.

'He's expected to get at least eleven seats in the state and cut into much of the OBC vote,' said Murugan. 'He is what you north Indians refer to as the vote *katua*, or someone who eats into the votes of the principal parties,' he added. Janaki nodded, Shashikanth was expected to get around 7 per cent of the vote—in a swing state, that was huge. He had, however, made powerful enemies among the granite and mining mafia, and security was tight.

A whir of helicopters was heard above and the crowd went a little wild, shouting out greetings to *karuppu arasan* (dark king), which is what Shashikanth was called.

Janaki felt a thrill go through her. She loved political reporting. It connected you to your country in a way little else did. She loved the mela of elections, the way issues were debated and even the scandals. She was often heard passionately arguing that politicians unfairly got a bad rap. Not starry-eyed in any way, of course, she was clear enough to know that politicians were not beings from Mars and were much like the other people of the country: bumptious, loud, emotional and contrary. They had that combination of naivety and native cunning that every Indian seemed to embody.

With hands raised over his head in a namaste, Shashikanth went up to the stage. The press enclosure was close to it, and his assistant Selvaraj motioned to Janaki that the interview was on. She sighed with relief, as that was one assignment Simran had wanted above all. 'And don't ask him political stuff, make it a colour piece about his favourite food, drink, colour, movies etc.,' she had said. 'Our readers don't watch his movies.'

As Shashikanth's booming voice resounded over the microphone, Janaki felt a frisson of unease, something she rarely felt. Her eyes scanned the adoring crowd; she could see nothing amiss. Suddenly, in the smallest of flashes, the world turned upside down.

~

In his office, Vishnu was swimming in files, things that had been sanctioned before the elections had been notified of course, when sudden red flashes of 'Breaking News' raced across the muted TV screen in his room. For a moment he was transfixed. 'Bomb blast at Shashikanth rally', read the ticker. He turned up the volume only to hear the words 'Shashikanth', 'bomb blast' and 'Madurai'. He was suddenly numb and then sick. He knew that Janaki was there.

'. . . police reports that casualty figures could climb further as the rally at Madurai's Panukkam grounds was jam-packed and the panic resulted in a stampede, which accounted for more deaths,' the anchor was saying.

Holy shit! thought Vishnu, *this can't be*! At once a picture of a blood-soaked body with Janaki's brandy eyes swam before his eyes. And I couldn't even apologize to her, he thought. He shook himself. He couldn't just stand there gaping and thinking silly thoughts. He had to do something! He pulled out his BlackBerry and called Sandeep Dwivedi, the district magistrate in Madurai. As expected, the line was engaged. He then called up Shankar Raghavan, his friend in the Chennai Intelligence Bureau. 'Hi Shankar, did you hear about Madurai? What's the scene like? Are you going there?' he asked anxiously, trying to sound not unusually alarmed.

'Yes, it seems that an interstate gang that has done this. Gross number of casualties, yaar! Now the rest of the elections will be a pain. Fortunately, the principal is unharmed and was whisked away from the site in his helicopter. The blast happened a little further on,' he said.

'And what about other people; was anyone from the press harmed? The TV is showing some garbled stuff,' said Vishnu.

'Don't know, I am going to the spot today. Going by road will be a pain; we are trying to organize an aircraft—there must be a hopping flight to Madurai,' Shankar said.

'Hmmm . . .' Vishnu said. 'Will you get the sanction?'

'The election commissioner and the chief minister are very concerned, especially since this is just a week before polling day. A helicopter could also be arranged,' said Shankar.

As Vishnu hung up, he decided to try Janaki's number. Scrolling through his phone, he dialled her number. He heard a strange series of clicks, like a phone disconnecting and then an ominous whir of static.

'Damn this blast!' he said. Without thinking, he called Venkataraman, his boss.

'Yes, Vishnu, what's the matter, my boy?'

'Sir, there has been a blast in Madurai, and I need to go there; is there any way we could swing it?' he asked urgently.

'Why? The home department guys will look after it; why should we finance guys be involved?'

Vishnu decided to make a clean breast of it. 'Sir, a friend of mine was at the site and I can't get through to her. I was supposed to look out for her . . .' he trailed off.

'Hmm . . . let me see what I can do. Is this friend really that special, eh?'

'Sir, please,' said Vishnu almost pleading.

'Okay, Okay, let me see. Weren't you DM in Madurai in your early years?'

'Yes sir, I was.'

~

Janaki could barely see through the haze of dust and crowds of people were scrambling around in panic. One minute she was looking at Shashikanth, and the next she was thrown to the ground as a tremor hit. Her first thought was that an earthquake had happened, and then the screaming started. Murugan dragged her through the press enclosure closer to where the helicopter stood. As they ran away from it, she had reason to be grateful to her new friend, for had she stayed in the press enclosure, she would have been trampled to death. They ran up a small elevation in the ground and watched. The bomb blast did not appear to be a high-intensity one, but they could see bodies strewn across the ground, children crying and people frantically searching for lost loved ones. Policemen was trying to get as many people away whichever way they could.

Both Murugan and Janaki fished out their notebooks; leaving the site was not an option. Janaki wrote down a description of what she saw, and started to inch back to the site. Several shell-shocked people were sitting up or lying down with blood-soaked hands and legs. That's when she realized that her hands were covered with blood too. A piece of shrapnel had found its way all the way to where she had been standing, digging into her extremities but fortunately leaving no critical injuries.

As ambulances and police vans made it to the spot, Janaki and Murugan spoke to some survivors to get their descriptions of the blast and what they saw before and after. No witness could recall anything out of the ordinary. Soon, first aid was being administered by emergency personnel who had rushed from Madurai's only government hospital, Rajaji Hospital, barely ten minutes away.

'There come the DM and SP,' said Murugan. As Janaki and Murugan inched their way to the district magistrate, he appeared irritated at the sight of them.

'I hope you people have received first aid,' he said at the sight of Janaki's bloodied arm.

'Yes sir,' she replied unconcerned. 'Sir, could you tell me of the expected number of casualties and the possible suspects behind the blast?' she asked. This was her moment to get as much information as possible. But the district magistrate was in no mood to oblige.

'Listen, lady, this is just a preliminary thing. We have to look at the site first, see the kind of explosive—why are you people always in such a goddamned hurry?' he asked.

Janaki left him alone after that, knowing that irritating him would not get her the information. She motioned to Murugan to follow her to the hospital. Working in Delhi, this situation was not new to her; if any casualty figures were to be had, the hospital would have a better idea than the government. Besides, there being only one government hospital, it narrowed the field somewhat.

Taking advantage of the confusion, Janaki and Murugan entered the hospital. People had occupied every available inch of space, and doctors and staff were running to and fro trying to cope with injuries, the injured and their relatives.

For the temple town of Madurai, home of the fish-eyed goddess Meenakshi, this was indeed a catastrophe.

The first thing they did was get their injuries seen to. Once the shrapnel was removed and her hand bandaged, Janaki followed some directions to the morgue. A beady-eyed mortician looked up as they entered his room; a register was open on his desk. Murugan started asking him questions in Tamil to find out the figures of those who had died and the nature of their injuries. They rapidly exchanged notes and the man motioned them to follow him.

As they entered the room, a tiny cubbyhole barely wide enough for three people to move around with any comfort, the sight which greeted Janaki made her gasp. The small morgue was horribly ill-equipped to deal with so many bodies! The seventeen dead had been stacked one on top of the other, awaiting identification.

The only other time Janaki had seen such a sight had been at the district hospital near Aligarh during a particularly vicious period of communal rioting. The smell of formaldehyde and blood permeated the room, and they quickly went outside again. She looked at her watch, which had cracked but still showed the time. Nearly three and a half hours had passed and Janaki realized that her office must have gone into panic mode. Thankfully her mother, living in Bangalore, didn't know that she was in Madurai today.

Janaki fished around in her handbag for her cellphone, she needed to call her office and tell them what had happened. That's when she realized that her phone had been smashed to pieces. 'Oh shit!' she exclaimed as she turned to Murugan. 'Listen, can I borrow your phone?'

Murugan fished out his phone and handed it to her, but it also seemed to be on the blink.

'Let's get to an STD booth,' she said. 'We've got the basic stuff; we can head out to the SP's or DM's office for some briefing after that,' she said.

As she stepped out of the hospital, a man came running towards her. 'Ms Janaki Rao? *Indian Mail*?' he said in heavily accented English.

'Yes.' Janaki looked surprised.

'DM saar wants to see you,' he said and asked her to follow him.

All was confusion at the district magistrate's office, but they were shown straightaway into Sandeep Dwivedi's office.

'Hello, please sit down,' he said to Janaki. 'Mr Venkataraman, the finance Secretary, called me and asked that I make sure that you were okay. I hope you've had the shrapnel seen to and got a tetanus shot?'

'Yes,' Janaki replied, frowning in confusion. She couldn't think of any reason the finance Secretary would be concerned about her. Her curiosity got appeased soon after.

'I'll ring up Vishnu Singh so you can just speak to him; apparently people from your office have been in touch with him over your safety,' he said as he dialled the number.

'Oh, that's the connection,' she thought sinking back into the chair, a soft smile on her face. So he had been concerned!

'Hello,' she said when the call connected.

'Hi, are you okay?' Vishnu asked, sounding extremely concerned.

'Yes, yes, I'm fine. We were near the podium; the blast was a little distance away.'

'Have you managed to book a cab to get back? I can arrange a car if you need it,' he said.

'What!' she said. 'No, no, I have to file from here, and then I leave for Coimbatore tomorrow. Please! I can't leave when the biggest news has broken here!' she said.

'Your office will allow this?' he asked incredulously. 'You've been in a bomb blast for crying out loud!'

'Mr Singh, I'm afraid that if I didn't stick around, there would be little point in my continuing in this profession. The vantage point I have is priceless,' she said.

'Well, all right then. Can you give the phone to Sandeep, please?' he said. After she gave him the phone Janaki watched as Dwivedi talked to Vishnu and kept stealing glances at her.

Disconnecting the call, he smiled at her. 'Well, are you still booked into a hotel here?' he asked. When she said yes, he asked if there was anything else she needed.

'Could I use your phone to call Delhi?' asked Janaki. She quickly dialled Simran's number and prayed that she would answer, despite the call being from an unknown number.

'Hello,' said Simran at the other end.

'Simran, hi, it's Janaki, calling from Madurai.'

The response was immediate. 'Oh my god! Janaki, are you okay? Your mother will kill me!' Simran had been taught in college by Janaki's mother, Professor Mythili Rao, before she retired.

'No, no, I'm fine. Just some scratches on my arm. I went to the hospital and have all the details; what do we do?'

'Well,' said Simran, back at her professional best, 'I want a first-person account, a spot story and an analysis of what it means for the elections. Keep each at 350 words, heavy ad pressure on the page.'

'So the usual, then. By the way, did Deepak get in touch with some guys in Chennai to check up on me?'

'I don't know. He's here; you ask him.'

'Hi Deepak. Did you ask Vishnu Singh to check if I was okay?'

'What? No yaar, I haven't spoken to him since I called him up to set up your meeting. Why? Is he piling on? You want me to kick his ass?'

'No, no, actually I was rather glad. He has been rather helpful,' Janaki responded and then hung up. Next, she dialled Saurabh's number, not knowing whether he would even be aware that she had been at the site of a bomb blast. As an independent documentary-maker, he kept late nights and even later mornings, his waking hours also coloured by a haze of pot.

'Hello, Saurabh, it's Janaki.'

'Arrey, whose number is this?' he said sleepily.

'My phone's on the blink. I was in a bomb blast. I'm okay now, don't worry,' she said and hung up. She had one last phone call to make, to her mother.

'Amma, it's Janaki. I'm in Madurai. I'm okay; my phone has conked off.'

Her mother asked her all the regular questions, satisfied herself that Janaki was unharmed and then hung up the phone.

Turning to the district magistrate, Janaki said, 'Mr Dwivedi, thank you very much. If you could help me with some information I will be out of your way soon.'

~

Vishnu stared at his phone for some time and decided that old man Venkataraman had been right. What was I thinking? he said to himself. I've just met her once; this is madness! I mustn't let my balls dictate to my brains! And yet, he would like to see her again. He wasn't sure what it was, but there was a connection. Life with her would be good, full of laughs, he thought.

Heaving himself out of his chair Vishnu stretched his back. His sedentary job was giving him a back problem. His phone rang and he saw Shashwati's number flash. Frowning, he picked up the phone. 'Hi, wassup?' he said casually. Their last meeting had been very dull, with both of them coming away with the feeling that this could be their last meeting.

'Hi,' Shashwati's voice came crackling down the wire. 'How are you? I called you before anyone else to say that I'm getting married next month in Kolkata,' she said in a rush.

'Well, congratulations! Who is the lucky guy?' His indifference secretly appalled him.

'His name is Sharath and he's handling an infrastructure firm in Hyderabad. We met through friends and now we're getting married.' It sounded rehearsed.

'Do you want me at your wedding?'

'Well, I'm not sure. He knows about us, so it will be a little awkward.'

Vishnu sighed. 'It's okay, yaar, I'll meet him later if you want. Have a good life. We had some fun times, didn't we?'

'That we did. But Vishnu, let someone in before you become unbreachable. Gayatri is not worth the pain.'

'Yeah, yeah. Maybe I'll take my chances with the hot maamis in Chennai,' he said with a laugh.

Later, at home, Vishnu stared almost meditatively at the Tanjore painting on the wall. Baby Krishna stared back at him innocently. What I need is a challenge, he thought. Maybe it's time for a mid-career refresher, a stint in college. Lately, mid-career bureaucrats were being sent to various universities in India and abroad for courses in various relevant fields.

Ramadin, a cook his mother had trained and planted in his household as her spy, came in with his beer and poppadums.

'Sir, the gardener wants chhutti for his wife's delivery. I have told him you will decide by tomorrow.'

'Arrey, tell him take the chhutti, Ramadin. Don't be such a martinet,' Vishnu said irritably.

Ramadin smirked and left him alone till it was time for dinner. Vishnu had picked up a fondness for the ultimate Tamilian comfort food, *thair saadham* (curd rice), and today he had a powerful need for it.

Four

'Can you please give me a bottle each of onion, tamarind and mint thokku,' said Janaki at the coupon counter at Grand Sweets. 'Half a kilo of coconut laddoo also, please.' It was late afternoon, and she had got back to Chennai that afternoon after a whirlwind, very productive professional tour. The sweets were a ritual with her, as was buying a sari. Her sari collection swelled with each trip outside Delhi: Maheshwaris, Chanderis, bagh prints, Benarsis—all being put away carefully. Today she would buy some Chettinad cottons and head to bed early because she was planning to leave Chennai on the first flight the next morning.

'Hi,' came a familiar voice from behind, a voice she heard often in her dreams.

'Hi,' she replied, a little breathless to see Vishnu so unexpectedly. 'Buying stuff for office?'

'Yeah.' Awkwardly she said, 'I was going to call you to thank you, but my phone, as you know . . .'

'Would you like to have dinner with me?' he asked suddenly, looking as surprised at the offer as Janaki, adding with a smile, 'and I remember it's supposed to be on me.'

Janaki caught her breath. Oh my! A dimpled chin; am I to have no mercy? she thought.

'Sure,' she said. 'I have to drop in to my office, and then I'm free.'

'Where do you want to go?'

'I don't know; it's your city.'

'We'll go to the East Coast Road. They have a nice band in one of the restaurants.'

'Okay. I'll be getting a cab, so I'll get there on my own.'

He nodded, named a restaurant and the exact location and left.

~

Janaki kept looking at the meagre wardrobe she had packed in a hurry for the trip. Sensible salwar kameezes, a pair of jeans, kurti tops and no heels. Shit, now what do I do? she thought. For some reason she wanted this man to remember her. 'How will I do that if I don't dazzle him?' she wailed. She quickly called Srividya. 'Listen, you need to get me a nice outfit and tell me a place where I can pick up a pair of heels, and, yes, a good parlour to get my hair done.'

'Whoa, whoa, hold on; what the hell is going on? Who the fuck has landed in Chennai to put you in such a tizzy?' Sri said, demanding her pound of flesh in info.

'Vishnu Singh has asked me out to dinner and for once I don't want to be the shabby journo.'

'Hmmm . . . okay. The clothes and parlour can be arranged, but what about your dear boyfriend back in Delhi?'

'It's just dinner, Sri, not a relationship, and I want to look my best—what's wrong with that?'

'Okay,' Sri said, naming several shops nearby for the shoes and clothes and the hair. Janaki decided to pick up a compact while out. A girl needs all the help she can get, she thought. She didn't want to examine too closely her reasons for wanting to dazzle the man—it was just enough that she wanted to.

~

Vishnu waited at the corner table feeling as nervous as a green young man. He had toyed with wearing a kurta, but changed his mind thinking it would be too much. In jeans and a formal shirt, he was looking at the entrance, when, bang on time, she arrived.

She cleans up nice, he thought. Janaki was wearing a long red skirt, sort of like a lehenga, with a fitted black T-shirt, and a red bandhini dupatta slung casually across. Strappy heels clicked on the tile flooring as she walked towards him, her hair a silky cloud around her face. Kohl-rimmed eyes brimmed with dark promises as she gave him a formal hug, her perfume musky and light at the same time.

Vishnu breathed deeply, storing it away in his mind. 'Hi,' he said, pulling out a chair for her before the waiter could get to it. They settled down and started ordering food. She was a vegetarian, and he was what he termed a 'committed carnivore'. They joked a little about it and ordered wine and dinner.

The conversation flowed easily; he spoke of his earlier years in the districts; she spoke of her days as a city reporter. He found her refreshingly without baggage, down to earth yet sophisticated and intelligent, even a bit of an intellectual, but without the ivory tower. Unfortunately, he also found out that she had a steady boyfriend, a filmmaker apparently. Sounds like a real chump, if she was mine I'd make sure I had married and branded her by now, he griped to himself.

They reached for the bottle wine at the same time, and their fingers brushed. Vishnu did not want to let go and stroked her palm with his index finger. Somehow their hands clasped and they continued talking, intensely aware of the clasped hands.

Oh my, this is a grown man, Janaki, don't make promises you can't follow through on, she thought. She gently disengaged her hand, but couldn't stop staring at his mouth. I wonder what it would be like to kiss him? she thought, then shook herself.

The dinner slowly ended and they both got up to leave. 'Where is your car?' he said. 'Let me drop you.'

'My driver is right outside the gate,' she said walking to the portico of the restaurant, the balmy ocean breeze mitigating the heat. She looked up at him and brushed his hair away from his forehead. 'Where is your car?' she asked suddenly.

The parking valet brought Vishnu's Honda City around and gave him the keys. Janaki got into the passenger seat. I have to do this; I cannot let him go without kissing him at least once, she thought. Oh my god, it must be the wine, she wailed to herself, even as he got into the car and gave her a puzzled look. As they pulled out of the restaurant and drove a little further, she asked him to stop the car.

He did. In the dark, she just looked at him, and her words whispered across the dark, 'Now let me kiss you.'

They leaned towards each other, Vishnu's hands clasping her face like a drowning man. Her nails raked across his back; her tongue duelled endlessly with his, and then she was nibbling at his lip, chin, jaw, and biting his earlobe. He groaned into her neck and bit the tender skin behind her ears. As suddenly as they came together they drew apart.

She looked at him and smiled. Patting his crotch, she asked, 'Are you okay?'

'Yes.' He laughed. 'Just don't ask me to get up any time soon!'

'I was very curious, you know . . . I just wanted to know what it would be like to kiss you. I normally never do this. It can't go any further.'

He sighed, tracing her eyebrow with a butterfly touch. 'It won't if you don't want it to. But why ever not?' He dropped little kisses on her eyelids and forehead.

Oh my! Janaki thought to herself. This is definitely a man, not a boy. 'I have plans. I love my boyfriend! I was just curious; I wanted to see how this would feel.'

'And how does it feel?'

She smiled at him and just said, 'I think you know.' Getting out of the car, she walked towards the car park they had left behind. Her cab driver saw her and drove towards her.

As Vishnu watched her leave he felt he had been punched in the gut. He had always been the one to do the wooing. And yet this girl had taken the lead and kissed the complacency out of him. 'Note to self, aggressive women are way hotter,' he said. He was surprised at the turn the evening had taken. He was not someone who was into forward women, and yet he found nothing vulgar about Janaki's moves. As graceful as a choreographed dance, he thought to himself. He recalled how he had had to persuade Gayatri at all times to even kiss him, and how she kept saying no, even if her body was screaming yes. He used to find that coyness and the body's betrayal as explosive as powder keg. And yet, now, Janaki had revealed what little he really knew about what he wanted.

He fished for his phone, wanting to talk to her, to tell her that she had taken his breath away, when he realized that she didn't have a phone—it had been destroyed in the bomb blast. Never mind, tomorrow morning I'll email her, he thought. Thank god for modern technology.

~

Janaki boarded the plane in a dreamlike state. She kept touching her lips, the little hickey on her neck and her eyebrows, where Vishnu's fingers had traced their way. This has to end here! You have plans that you have been making since you were in college, and they do not involve bachelors in their thirties even if they have dimpled chins, she said to herself. Ooohhh, what he must think of me, that I put out for every guy!!!

She berated herself throughout the flight, ending up feeling so guilty for having betrayed her boyfriend that, when she saw him at the arrivals gate of the airport holding a bunch of wilted roses, she wept. 'Hey, I know, I know that bomb blast was really too much,' said Saurabh, 'but, Janu, please get a grip. People are staring; they probably think I beat you or something!'

Janaki sniffed, rubbed her eyes and asked, 'Where's the cab?' At this Saurabh started grinning. 'Ta da,' he said, and a new Hyundai i20 swept up the drive, complete with a driver. 'What's this?' she asked. Saurabh cared too much for his status as a struggling artist to roam around in swanky cars.

'I just got hired to do camerawork on a commissioned serial on Doordarshan, and bought this,' he said.

'Saurabh, you know that we are saving up to buy a house for when we are married.'

'Arrey, a little indulgence is good!'

Janaki knew that the car would soon be gone, like many of the other good things bought on expectations. With Saurabh she constantly felt like an older sister cautioning him on profligate ways. Oh fuck it, what does it matter, she said to herself as she loaded her suitcase.

As the car deposited her at La Vista apartments in the eastern suburbs of the city, she picked up her mail from the society office and asked the guard to locate Jyotsna, her maid. She opened the door to shedding leaves. 'Oh no,' she said. 'Saurabh, why didn't you water my money plant?'

'Arrey yaar, isse tumhe asli money thodi aajayega!' he said in that indifferent way of his. 'Want me to make some khichdi?'

'No, please go now, I have to do a lot of cleaning, come over in the evening.'

'Er, Javed might drop in as well.'

'Look, I'm too tired. I'll see you tomorrow then, okay?' she said and firmly shut the door. Saurabh never travelled anywhere without an entourage; in the beginning it appeared to be fun, but now it was plain irritating.

As Jyotsna came in, Janaki quickly cleaned up the house and sent her off to stock up on vegetables and milk. Tomorrow is Thursday, may have to go in to work, she thought to herself.

It was only in the evening that she managed to turn on her laptop. As she logged into Gmail, her heart skipped a beat. On her screen, lordvishnu@gmail.com had sent her a chat request. She acquiesced and waited to see if he was online. He wasn't. Well, thank god for small mercies, she thought and quickly checked some press releases and logged out.

Janaki had by now completely convinced herself that Vishnu would think that she was a slut. I shouldn't have kissed him, at least I would have had my dignity intact, she told herself.

~

The big news of the day was an impending cabinet reshuffle, and *Indian Mail*'s newsroom was buzzing. Kishore Mukherjee, their managing editor, was having his weekly powwow with the political bureau and, except for this piece of news, nobody had anything to contribute. Janaki tried to soften the editor with some coconut laddoos, but his blood sugar had been high in last week's check-up and Kishoreda was trying to be good.

Deepak, the sod, had already tried the 'urgent phone call' trick and weaselled out of the meeting. 'Sir, I have a meeting with a source,' he said. Since Deepak covered the intelligence agencies, Kishoreda nodded enthusiastically and did not enquire as to who this source was. 'Saala, there is no source-worce, he's skipped out to Udipi and is probably having coffee with Manoj Nair and planning their next daaru bender,' Janaki's best friend in the office, Monika Agarwal, whispered.

Janaki nodded. She also had this really painful instinct that she would be asked to write a long Sunday piece on the election trail. Well, there is only one way to avoid it, she thought. 'Sir,' she said, 'Chennai is the best place to pick up movies and books; Delhi is a village compared to their stores.' And then she threw her brahmastra. 'In fact, the local Landmark had a huge collection of Ghatak movies,' she said.

'Really!' he exclaimed immediately. 'Did you pick up any?' Kishoreda was a die-hard Ritwik Ghatak fan and, in disastrous meetings, Ghatak could always be counted on to distract him.

'Only *Meghe Dakha Tara* and *Komal Gandhar*, sir,' she said. 'Although I find his sensibilities too masculine for my taste.'

Cramming for the Jamia MCRC programme had made her comfortable with some jargon. From the corner of her eye she could see Prithvi Singh, their CBI correspondent nod knowledgeably; Janaki barely stifled a laugh. The closest that the alpha male Prithvi could have gotten to someone named Ghatak was if he was in the CBI net. As Kishoreda launched into how Ghatak was the most underrated moviemaker in history and Ray the most overrated, the management guys trooped in for their meeting.

As notebooks were shut and people shuffled away, Simran sidled up to Janaki. 'Smart; took one for the team. By the way, you can't wiggle out of your primary responsibility.'

'What's that?' Janaki asked.

'My column. I'm writing on the new education policy, you have to dig up some dirt on the minister. And till Daisy Duck is back you have to look at the allies of the National Secular Alliance government, which means that the reshuffle story is your baby. Now get cracking.' Daisy Duck was what Simran called Shakira, whose divine backside had given her a peculiar waddle as well.

'But Simran, I have to get a phone and file a police complaint to get my SIM replaced,' wailed Janaki.

Simran simply turned and called out to the telecom and crime reporters from their sections. 'Help her; she needs to be connected in a day. And George,' she said to the telecom reporter, 'your next increment will depend on whether this gets done.'

George Paul, a phlegmatic Malayali, laughed at that. 'Are you actually saying we may get an increment this year; can I quote you?' he asked and, not waiting for answer, turned his attention to Janaki. 'Anyway, Janaki, I'll hook you up with that Nokia guy, you know the one who said he could hear your inner ringtone,' he said with a mischievous look.

'That stalker, don't you dare!' Janaki threatened him. He laughed.

Sure enough, by the evening her phone was resurrected, and she had even recovered some numbers, but she was nowhere close to cracking the reshuffle story. As she logged on to Gmail, she barely glanced at the chat list when suddenly there it was.

lordvishnu: hi

Oh my, thought Janaki. Now what do I do? Well, here goes.

me: hi
lordvishnu: long radio silence huh?
me: lord vishnu? really? nothing else was available?
lordvishnu: :) do you know how many vishnu singhs are there on the world wide web?
me: hmmm . . . still . . .
lordvishnu: anyway, i guessed you don't kiss and tell, but i didn't know you didn't kiss and talk either . . .
me: omg please don't remind me . . . u have to know that i never do this kind of thing!!! u r the first new guy i have kissed in five years . . . u must think i'm a slut . . .
lordvishnu: not at all . . . i can't get it out of my mind . . . i can't get over how graceful you were . . . the way u whispered . . . now let me kiss u . . .
me: please just stop this. the best thing i can think of is that u r in chennai and i am here.
lordvishnu: i may not be in chennai long, what if i turn up in delhi?
me: don't even joke about this . . .
lordvishnu: in fact this is a scoop for you . . . i will be in town as the new commerce minister purushottamam's private secretary . . .
me: wow . . . so he is the new inductee . . . i won't quote u but is this completely true . . .
lordvishnu: yes . . . huge promotion for me . . . and now u will have no more excuses :)
me: what's this guy's background?
lordvishnu: google has it all . . . but very pro-farmer . . .

me: ok gotta go . . .tks for the scoop, u saved my job . . . i owe u 1 . . .

lordvishnu: don't worry, i'll collect . . .

Janaki raised her eyebrows at that and logged out. Sure enough Google had all clippings related to Purushottamam that she needed, how he was one of the contenders to take over the Tamil Nationalist Front which was in power in the state and was expected to retain power in these assembly elections. His move to Delhi meant either that a succession plan had been worked out or that he had decided to play for bigger stakes from Delhi.

She almost ran the distance between her seat and Simran's cabin. Simran was on the phone, but waved Janaki in.

'Well, we've cracked it, the reshuffle will see D. Purushottamam as the new commerce minister, which means that, if the TNF comes to power again, Jayaraman will be CM, and Purushottamam will handle Delhi,' she said almost out of breath soon after Simran had put down the phone and given her a questioning look.

Simran told her to sit down and asked her the source of the information. 'Deepak's friend Vishnu told me he is coming here as Purushottamam's private secretary,' she said. 'But he has asked me not to quote him. Simran held up her hand and dialled a number from her cellphone.

'Sirji, this is Simran Kher from *Indian Mail*. Sir, you never make time for me any more,' she said coyly as Janaki watched, bemused. 'Sirji, what is this I'm hearing?' continued Simran, eventually wheedling a confirmation on Janaki's story.

'Okay, attribute it to top government sources, and give the padding to the copy about the succession plan in the TNF. Not more than a tight 350 words; I'll pitch for page 1. But I want it before the evening meeting. Well done! With a WTO ministerial meeting scheduled in Hong Kong next month to discuss agriculture, a pro-farmer commerce minister would be huge.'

It was with a great deal of pleasure that Janaki perused the morning papers the next day. Sipping her tulsi tea, Janaki saw that only the *Indian Mail* had the story. She knew, even as she peacefully sipped her tea, that there were many angry phone calls to beat reporters from the bureau chiefs of various papers, demanding explanations for how they missed the story. Someone had once very memorably said that a reporter's happiness and satisfaction was directly proportionate to the number of beat reporters who were shafted because of his or her story. There ought to be several reporters who won't be able to sit down today, thought Janaki with great satisfaction.

Though, that was yesterday; what's the story today, she wondered. May and June were usually the silly season for news and, sure enough, as Janaki called her various sources she found that many of them were on jaunts abroad. And we're stuck here in bloody fucking Delhi, she thought.

As Simran called her for the story list, Janaki decided to spoil their fun. 'How about a story on all these ministers and PAs on foreign jaunts, escaping the summer on taxpayer money. Some of these jaunts are simply excuses to escape the heat, like the minister for animal husbandry going to Switzerland to see cows mate.'

Simran cackled at the other end. 'Accha hai; make it spicy; could be pitched for bottom of the front page anchor.'

As she hung up, Janaki saw that she had a missed call from Saurabh. A now familiar pang of guilt shot through her as she dialled his number. 'Hi, good morning sweetness,' she said.

'Hi,' he said sleepily, 'congrats on the page 1; cracker of a story.'

Janaki felt like a heel for even thinking about another man. Saurabh and she had been together for so long and they had held hands through a lot.

'How about you come over and I make some great rajma chawal for you?' he said.

'Great, I'll be in around nineish.'

'I also wanted to say that I'm sorry if I upset you over the car. I know you feel that your Wagon R should be enough, but I needed one too.'

Janaki felt a little irritated at that. I'm not his mum, she thought to herself. 'Listen, it's quite all right, it's your money after all. And our plans were not set in stone.'

'Are you sure?'

'Yes.'

'I've also bought a Nikon camera; she's a beauty, you ought to see her,' he said excitedly.

Janaki sighed, wondering if her fate was to play the heavy. 'Okay, I'll see you in the evening. Do you want me to bring some booze?'

'Nope, Sukumar said he had some Finlandia vodka from his trip to Dubai; just bring yourself.'

Saurabh lived just a few blocks away. They could have moved in together, but somehow Janaki had resisted till now. She wanted her own space. She liked hanging out with Saurabh, but she liked coming back to her place even better. Saurabh lived in a chaotic way, with friends in and out of the house at all times. Though the house was neat, it did not reflect his maverick character; that was reserved for his work and friends, the house was just incidental. Janaki, on the other hand, had bought and even restored some of the furniture in her house herself. Curtains, rods and even bathroom sinks had been refitted to her specifications. She was house-proud, no doubt about it.

~

Vishnu surfed the net and caught the national edition of the *Indian Mail*, with Janaki's story as a flyer on page 1. If that doesn't get me brownie points, nothing will, he thought to himself. He was not in the business of planting stories or betraying scoops, but this was quite harmless.

Vishnu had routinely gone to meet Venkataraman two days after Janaki had left. 'Well, my boy, I have some good news for you. Purushottamam is very happy with your work here and is on the lookout for a principal secretary when he goes to Delhi as commerce minister. This will be a huge assignment, you will be stepping over at least fourteen senior people, but it will fast-track you like nothing else,' he said.

Vishnu did not need to be convinced; he was ambitious to the core and Venkataraman had never failed him. And, while bureaucracy was all about structure and hierarchy, the top of the pyramid was reserved for people for whom exceptions were made.

'Sir, this could be the best thing that has happened to me! I'm really very grateful, sir.' He didn't know why the old man had taken to him, but was just happy that the gods were smiling on him.

'By the way, the young lady in Madurai, Dwivedi told me she was a plucky lass, journalist apparently, and filed stories for the paper despite injuries.'

'Yes sir.' Vishnu blushed.

'Good, good. She is in Delhi I believe. Interesting,' said Venkataraman and left it at that. 'Please go and meet Purushottamam for breakfast tomorrow, and start packing for Delhi.'

Vishnu went home with mixed feelings. He was a go-getter when it came to his career, but, when it came to his personal life, he had let things drift. He was comfortable in his cocoon in Chennai; apart from the summer it was a nice city. Now he was to go back to the city where he had spent his student days. Well, into the breach, he thought to himself.

~

Janaki was having a ball in the summer; a short reshuffle had completely authenticated her story and she was confident that she was in for a good appraisal, albeit a little in the future. Plus the whole pleasure of aggravating Shakira was just too delicious. 'Janaki, I don't think your information is correct. Rajshekharan from *Dinasitara* told me that there was no way in hell Purushottamam would agree to come to Delhi,' she had cooed at Janaki.

Janaki had ignored her and, sure enough, the reshuffle saw

Purushottamam make it as commerce minister. She managed to catch a glimpse of Vishnu, but Monika, who was their official commerce ministry reporter, had said that Purushottamam would only be available during the monsoon session of Parliament.

In the meantime, Saurabh had got some good assignments and was talking of taking a vacation in the hills. 'We'll go to Landour, yaar, with some friends, guitar-witar bajayenge, daaru peeyenge and mast rahenge,' he said happily.

Janaki was tempted to escape the heat and put in a leave application. First dibs on vacation time were of course for people with children, summer vacations having begun. However, she was on the road to the hills in a short while. As a journalist, the only perk she thought she got was booking government guest houses for vacations. As they climbed out of the hot plains their spirits lifted, and it was a very merry party of seven people who reached Landour.

The air was crisp, Saurabh was his usual fun self and Janaki made serious inroads into her reading. As the five days of vacation went by Janaki rarely thought of Vishnu except when an occasional breeze caressed her, and she thought of his soft tender hands.

Five

'Parliament is a prison,' Janaki thought to herself as she went through the several levels of security checks required to get into the building. There was also something collegiate about Parliament, the drama of the two Houses and debates mirroring a classroom, with the country as audience and judge. It was also a boon for reporters because, four times a year, all the major politicians of the country were somehow trapped in the building with the national media. Networking became much easier; information exploded out of the building.

Janaki trudged in with her 'parliament shoes': flat sandals with a lot of wear on them, since she easily clocked two kilometres a day in the circular building, trying to keep track of major developments, meeting people and collecting elusive government reports.

The Delhi sky was leaden with clouds, which was good news as summer had been particularly cruel that year. As she hefted her hold-all handbag onto her shoulder, Janaki was hit by a prickle of awareness that she was being watched. It was common in Parliament to see groups of journalists surrounding an MP or minister chatting him or her up as they waited for their cars at the portico. Most times Janaki paid little attention to them; this time, however, she did a quick scan of the crowds outside the Rajya Sabha entrance at Gate no. 2 of Parliament. And then she saw him.

Oh my god, she said to herself as her eyes locked with Vishnu's. Her panicked stare contrasted too vividly with his amused 'gotcha' look. His boss, Purushottamam, was holding court as the new minister, with journalists surrounding him. Vishnu stood a little way back and continued to stare at Janaki for a while. Then he broke away from the group and loped over to her on his long legs.

'Hi. How have you been?'

'Fine,' Janaki croaked at him, and then bit her lip in embarrassment. Why god, why? she wailed to herself. But man, he looks sooo good. Preppy men had not been her style at all, only artsy ones, but this one . . . she shook herself and commanded all the dignity she could.

'Hi, how have you been? Have you settled in?' she asked, taking in all the details of his appearance, including the dimpled chin. Still as hot as ever, she thought miserably, suddenly aware that her work uniform of a short kurti and comfy jeans gave her as much appeal as a wet rag.

'Yeah, I have a house in South Extension, and have decided to stay there instead of the official quarters. I have been meaning to call you, but as you know, you never gave me your new number,' he said with a mocking smile.

'Umm, well, I'll remedy the situation right now,' she said with an apologetic smile. She rattled out her number and hoped and prayed that this was not the beginning of him hounding her.

'Also, I need to collect on the scoop I gave you,' he said with a smile, and Janaki's composure vanished with a whimper.

'Look, I know my behaviour has been quite forward, but I don't do that kind of thing. It was something out of the blue. I don't know what you're expecting, but let me tell you, it ain't happening,' she said in a huff, acutely aware that she was surrounded by all her peers.

'I only expect you to have one drink with me. I don't do this kind of thing either, but we had a connection and, no, I don't think of you as just an easy lay,' he said, vocalizing her own reservations. 'This is not a good place to have this conversation; I'll call you in the evening, okay?'

She nodded mutely, the temptation to reach up and run her fingers through his hair was enormous.

'And please, for god's sake, stop looking at me like that; it's becoming difficult to keep standing,' he added with a grin.

Janaki frowned quickly and turned and walked away in embarrassment, straight into her friend Monika Agarwal.

'Whoa, whoa, hold on there! I didn't know you knew this guy.' Monika said, flashing a smile at Vishnu. Since she covered the commerce ministry, knowing the minister's private secretary would be invaluable for her. She nudged Janaki, who reluctantly made the introductions.

'Sir, I was wondering when I could come and meet you,' Monika asked immediately. 'There were some things I needed to clarify for a curtain raiser on the next WTO meet.'

'Why don't you and Janaki come over for tea on Friday. The minister will also not be on Parliament roster, so you guys can be introduced as well,' Vishnu said with a charming smile.

'Oh, that would be great!' Monika said, completely missing the panicked look Janaki sent her.

As Vishnu turned and walked away a loud shriek was heard.

'Vishnu Singh, you handsome rogue, you!' came Shakira Banerjee's unmistakable cooing tones. 'Don't tell me you were going to walk away without saying hi,' she said and proceeded to do the air-kiss, leaning into Vishnu, who now had the expression of a hunted rabbit. 'Why, you never told me you were going to be in Delhi, and we are such old friends.'

Janaki could barely suppress her laughter at Vishnu's stricken expression. 'Well, I should leave you two old friends alone. Anyway, the debate on price rise is about to start,' she said and ran for her life.

But she had reckoned without the eagle-eyed Monika. 'Okay, give over,' said Monika. 'I haven't been married that long that I forget what a smitten guy looks like,' she said. 'What is going on?' As both cleared security yet again they huddled in a deserted part of the corridor. 'Tell all,' Monika demanded imperiously.

'Well, I met him when I went there to cover the elections, you know. He was very helpful when the bomb blast happened and all. We went out to dinner . . .' she trailed off.

'And,' prompted Monika.

'And I kissed him,' Janaki said letting out her breath in a whoosh.

'Wow! So how was it?'

Janaki sputtered in surprise. 'What's this, no moral outrage?'

'What's the use, you've already done the deed, so how was it?' Monika asked matter-of-factly.

'It was magical.' Janaki sighed. 'But I don't think I should have done it.'

'Why?'

Monika had somehow not taken to Saurabh much. She was convinced that his bohemianism came at great cost to Janaki, who was always expected to pick up the pieces, pitch in with money when jobs were lost due to temper tantrums and constantly cheer his chosen fraught career. 'So you would prefer to toil on with a guy who obviously takes you for granted instead of exploring something else?' she asked, in her infinite wisdom.

'C'mon Mon, he and I come from different worlds! He is much older and a hidebound bureaucrat, you know what I feel about these entitled sods,' replied Janaki. As a journalist she dealt with bureaucrats every day, but did not always find the experience very pleasant. The sense of entitlement that many of the class I officers went around with was particularly galling to her. Journalism will make a socialist of me yet, she always said to herself.

Monika saw that arguing with Janaki was going to be futile. 'Well, at least string him along so I can get a few scoops,' she said with a laugh.

Janaki laughed too, knowing that the prudish Monika had not meant the suggestion seriously.

Six

Janaki stared at herself in the mirror, at the demure salwar kameez she had put on after her bath, and jokingly wondered whether she should substitute it with a nun's habit. I think this should convince the guy that I'm not putting out at any time, she thought to herself.

It was Friday, and although they were not scheduled to meet Vishnu and his boss till at least 4 p.m., Janaki had to cover the morning session of Parliament before she went on to other appointments. Fridays were considered light days while covering Parliament as after 2.30 p.m., the house went on to private members' business, which meant MPs moved private bills which had no party backing and reflected their own individual, and sometimes eccentric, concerns. The press usually ignored these proceedings, as did the majority of MPs, who used the early escape from Parliament to travel back to their constituencies for the weekend.

Vishnu had told Monika that Purushottamam was also scheduled to travel back to Chennai by the late evening flight. As Janaki breezed through the day, at the back of her mind was a vague sort of apprehension over seeing Vishnu again.

Just my luck! One guy I kiss for a lark, saala turns up here, she muttered to herself. Thomas Mathew, reporter for *Daily Hindustan*, who was walking beside her through Nirman Bhavan, the building which housed the health and urban development ministries, stopped short and said, 'Huh?! You said something?'

Before she could answer, her phone buzzed. It was Monika, who said that she was waiting for her in the anteroom of Purushottamam's office at Udyog Bhavan.

'I'll be right there,' Janaki said as she rushed across to the adjacent building, which housed his office, and then cursed herself for it. Now I'll be all sweaty again. Nothing for it; it's my fate, I can never be cool enough around him, she thought as she approached the office in her vanity heels.

When she reached the anteroom, Monika wasn't there, but a peon waved her into Vishnu's office. Janaki held her breath and entered. Monika and Vishnu were seated on a couch drinking tea, and at first sight appeared to be getting along just fine without her.

'Hi!' Vishnu said and got up as she entered. 'Come, sit down,' indicating a chair nearby. As she settled herself and surreptitiously patted her hair in place, he opened what looked like a masala box with a flourish. 'So, what kind of tea would you like?'

Janaki, who swore by Indian masala tea, preferably with ginger and cooked to within an inch of its life, looked blankly at the box where a bewildering array of tea bags greeted her.

'Er . . . you choose,' she said and shut her mouth.

Vishnu gave her a puzzled look and said, 'The choosing of a tea is a delicate business. Could I presume to do that?'

Just give me some goddamn tea already, thought Janaki, and then realized with a start that she'd said it aloud. 'Um . . . I'm sorry,' she said pleadingly while Monika quietly choked over her cup of oolong in a corner.

Vishnu frowned, and then chose some regular jasmine tea and went through what appeared to Janaki as an almost prissy ceremonial process of making her a cup. Sheesh, she thought, now that's high maintenance.

'Here,' said Vishnu, handing her a cup of what she termed glorified hot water.

'So what do you cover?' he asked Monika. As the three of them chatted about this and that, the ten-minute wait flew past and soon they were ushered into the minister's chambers.

'Namaste,' said Purushottamam, and waved them to a couple of chairs opposite his desk. As the informal introductions were made, cards handed out and a small question–and–answer session started, Janaki surreptitiously glanced at Vishnu, who kept prompting his boss on facts and figures in response to Monika's questions.

Janaki's more political questions were handled by the wily Purushottamam himself. As Janaki finished up with the meeting, she glanced at her phone and noticed some SMS alerts. She checked her messages as they exited the chambers.

'Hi, wanna meet up for a drnk, arnd 7?' Vishnu's SMS glowed as though laid out in neon lights. Janaki didn't know what to say. The honest truth was she wanted to meet him very badly, but two things prevented her from saying yes.

'And what are those two reasons,' asked Monika as they discussed it on the way back to ITO, where their office was.

'First, he probably thinks I'm easy because I kissed him, and will make this obvious and piss me off tonight, and second, I'm not dressed for it!' Janaki hated that she lived far from work and could never be decently turned out for evening engagements unless she carried clothes and make-up with her and changed in the office loo.

'I find it very interesting that neither of these reasons you give has anything to do with the fact that you already have a boyfriend,' said Monika speculatively. 'Hmmm, good, my child, you are making progress,' she said with an impish smile.

Monika's remarks struck Janaki like a thunderbolt. In all of her agonizing soul searching she hadn't once thought of Saurabh. It's like he's not in my life any more! she thought. That really brought her up short.

~

As he watched the two women walk away, Vishnu was swamped by mixed feelings. Janaki was as appealing as before, but he clearly made her uncomfortable.

However, as he battled the city's traffic to South Extension, where he lived, Janaki was far from his mind. For today he was coming home to his mother: the formidable Indira Singh, known to reduce grown men to tears with a flick of her patrician eyebrows.

As he walked into the house, he could see Ramadin whispering to his mother, probably giving her the lowdown on everything, even his bloody bowel movements, he thought disgustedly to himself. I have sold my soul for Ramadin's kebabs and biryani, he thought, and not for the first time.

'Beta, come and give your mother a hug. It's been a while since I saw you,' his mother said to him.

Vishnu dutifully went over and did as he was bid. His mother continued, 'I hope you are feeling up to going out. Mrs Srivastava has invited us to dinner this Saturday. You remember Piu, her daughter? She is just back from England after completing her law degree, so they are hosting a welcome back dinner.'

Vishnu had known he would be lassoed into some of the social whirl his mother loved, but didn't expect it to be so soon. Indira Singh's life was one social engagement after another or, as his father used to say jokingly, 'No birth, death or marriage can even hope to be acknowledged unless your mother is there.'

'Ma,' Vishnu groaned. 'You know I go to Siri Fort Club to play squash on Saturdays, and you know how tough it is to get the court!'

Just then his phone beeped an SMS alert. 'Sorry. Not tonight. Raincheck?' read Janaki's message. That put him in an even more foul mood.

After dinner, as he settled down at his computer and what he called 'me time', he was a little taken aback to see a very familiar email address blink back at him. Gayatri Kaul Dhar, he read. As he opened her message, his hand shook a bit.

The contents of the message were an even bigger shock.

Hi
I know it's been a long time since we were in touch, but I heard that you are in Delhi now. I am also here, in economic

affairs. Would it be possible, do you think, for us to meet? So that if we do bump into each other, it won't be awkward?

Gayatri.

Vishnu's first instinct was to say no. But he was forced to admit to himself that he wanted to see her again. Her profile picture on Facebook gave little away. I hope she's fat! he thought viciously. Really huge! So I get over her fast enough!

He wrote back.

Hi

Surprised to hear from you after such a long while. Of course we can meet up. Please state your convenience and we will work something out. How is Pramod? And your son?

Affly
Vishnu.

There, he thought to himself. Into the breach once again, my friends.

~

Vishnu and 'Piu', aka Priyanka Srivastava, looked at each other sympathetically. Both had quite obviously been paired up, and neither had any intention of making their respective mothers any happier.

'I'm sorry, but you look too much like my mother, so there is no way we're getting together,' said Vishnu apologetically.

'Hey, you are no oil painting either,' she said. 'No offence,' she added sticking out her tongue at him. 'So how do we wriggle out of this one?'

'Well, I have a prior engagement. If you can stick it out for fifteen minutes more, you will be rid of me,' he said with a smile, not for the first time wondering to himself why he couldn't just simplify his life and fall for a girl like Priyanka.

Coolly ignoring his mother's frantic waves for him as he sidled out of the Srivastava home in Greater Kailash, Vishnu flashed a dimpled smile at his co-conspirator. 'Maybe when we're not being thrown at each other like this, we can meet for a coffee and actually be friends,' he said.

'I like the sound of that,' said Priyanka.

Driving towards Khan Market for his dreaded meeting with Gayatri, Vishnu felt his heart thudding. 'What the fuck, after so many years, I cannot frigging believe it,' he muttered. Parking at Khan Market was the usual test of patience and endurance, requiring a certain chutzpah that only Delhiwallahs seemed to possess.

Finally finding a good spot, he slid out of his car and made his way to a local pub. As usual, crowds of young people hung around Khan Chacha's, gorging on kebabs, and Vishnu picked his way around them. As he entered the pub, he scanned the crowd for Gayatri. Instead of his glacial ex-girlfriend, he encountered the sultry Janaki, holding court at a corner table with what looked like a gang of salivating men. So she only says no to me, is it? he muttered to himself. All thoughts of Gayatri flew from his mind.

Before he realized it, Vishnu had stalked up to Janaki. 'Hi,' he said. 'How come you are here?' he asked, almost wincing at his jealous tone, realizing belatedly that Monika was there too, and eyeing him with a gleam in her eye that clearly said that she was on to him.

A flush crept up Janaki's face and she stuttered her response. 'Oh, hi Vishnu, meet Saurabh. Monika you know and that is Manoj, Monika's husband.'

Vishnu nodded at all of them, feeling ashamed at his behaviour. He looked at Saurabh, sizing him.

'Wassup?' Saurabh asked in that casual way of his.

'Hello,' said Vishnu. I could sooo take him, he thought happily, noting that Saurabh was a typical young male in arrested development mode, still dressed in college togs. Just one fight dude, we'll be done, he thought to himself, and then winced in horror at his thoughts. He nodded at the long-haired Saurabh and at Manoj, who shared his wife's knowing look.

'Hi!' said a female voice in dulcet tones behind him, and Vishnu, irritated, turned around to come face to face with Gayatri. Oh shit, he thought to himself, I can't believe I actually forgot I came here to meet Gayatri!

'Hi,' he said.

With a wave of her hand Gayatri gestured that they get to a table fast. Perversely, Vishnu wanted to linger, but realized it wasn't a wise move. He said goodbye to Janaki, who had raised one eyebrow at Gayatri's dismissive move.

As Vishnu and Gayatri settled down at their table, he couldn't help being aware that Janaki was still there, her glowing presence like a hand stroking down his back. With an effort he drew his attention back to Gayatri. 'So, how have you been?' he asked, even as he realized that the one thing he feared was no longer a threat. He felt nothing in her presence except a profound relief that he was free of her cold beauty.

Sitting four tables away, Janaki miserably noted the beautiful woman seated with Vishnu. I bet she never sweats, she thought to herself, and if she does, it must be in demure driblets reeking of Chanel. If that's his type, he ain't never going to go for you, she continued on a masochistic self-pity track that only Saurabh's usual drunk tantrum managed to snap her out of.

The waiter had called out last orders for happy hours, and Saurabh wanted to drink some more, while Monika and Manoj wanted to go home. The couple had been trying for a baby for some time, and clean living and sex by timetable were a top priority now, something Saurabh just didn't seem to get. 'Arrey, here is a jar, put your balls in it and just give it to Monika, man. End the farce of free will in marriage,' he said tauntingly to Manoj.

Manoj looked furious and got up to leave, Monika shot an apologetic look at Janaki who, for once, refused to pick up the flak for Saurabh's behaviour. This is the outside of enough, she thought. 'Saurabh, please apologize to Manoj and stop behaving like a jerk.' Saurabh looked at her sheepishly and apologized to Manoj, who simply nodded and walked off. Monika looked back at Janaki with her own apologetic look. Janaki by then had had enough. 'Dude, this is just crap. I don't think I can take this any more. Find your own way home,' she said and walked off, not even bothering to check whether Saurabh was following her.

Saurabh trailed after her, thinking that this was just one of the many scraps they had got into in the past. 'Arrey yaar, why are you getting pissed off?' he said. 'Yeh to chalta rahta hai.' But Janaki was furious, and for some reason it had a lot to do with the man at the back of the pub—a man who was probably thanking his stars that he wasn't with her, Janaki thought miserably to herself. 'Just forget it, I'm going home, I suggest you go home too,' she said and got into her car.

Seven

It was a very bemused Vishnu who settled into his chair in the office on Monday morning. The meeting with Gayatri on Saturday night had been, to say the least, surreal. He felt quite unaffected by her, even though she looked much the same as when they were together; her beauty was just as compelling and her mannerisms just as commanding of attention. It isn't her, it's me, he thought, chuckling to himself at the cliché.

Gayatri had been very candid with him about what she had been up to since they'd stopped talking, her postings in the districts, her son Amol and her husband Pramod, for whom she appeared to have only thinly disguised contempt.

'I was wrong, Vishnu, to have chosen to marry for convention,' she said. She clung to his fingers; Vishnu could barely draw his hands away.

'We all have to live with the choices we make,' he said, and cringed at the banal phrase. He was acting deliberately obtuse; he wanted to savour the liberation from Gayatri, a novel feeling for him.

'You have no idea about the consequences of that decision, Vishnu.'

Vishnu may have been in Janaki's thrall at the moment, but this vulnerable side of Gayatri still took hold of him.

'Gayatri, are you sure you want to tell me all this?'

'Vishnu, I don't know who else to turn to,' she said. And the whole tale of her marriage to Pramod Dhar came tumbling out. It had started out fine, but then, once the child came along and Gayatri and Pramod got busy with their careers, came the pain and the fights and the affairs. 'He got involved with his PS, and I know a couple of other instances where he has been with other women,' she said, tears welling up in her eyes. He had held her hand then. Although he didn't feel drawn to her like he had been, he couldn't help but feel a tug at his heart.

Vishnu had also decided last night, after spending the evening intensely aware of Janaki, that he had to take charge of the situation there. He wanted her, and had decided to throw scruples to the winds. This one is not going to get away, he said to himself. He also decided that, in this relationship at least, he would set the pace. He would say when and where, and if she didn't like it then too bad.

He quickly dialled Janaki's number. 'Hello,' came a brusque voice at the end of the line, and Vishnu said, 'Hi, it's Vishnu here. My god, you are curt on the phone.'

'Oh, sorry, it's just that I'm getting out of the door and have had too many calls offering me personal loans,' came the breathless reply.

Vishnu smiled to himself. 'Well, are you ready to take the rain check on that drink today?'

'Umm . . . sure, why not? Do you know the Leaping Frog at Khan Market; we can meet there around, say, eight?'

'Eight at Khan it is.' As he hung up the phone, he told himself that he would be careful this time round.

~

Janaki got off the phone and rushed back in to pack a fresh top and some make-up for the evening. After last night she had realized that Saurabh and she were over. She had never believed in love at first sight, and now she wasn't even sure if there was any one person out there for her. She had met Saurabh at a totally different time in her life. She was twenty-eight now, had been working for five years and in a profession where she met different sorts of people, and had become fiercely independent. Saurabh's goals were different and his self-indulgence was not something she planned to take on for the rest of her life. Meeting Vishnu had clarified that in her mind. Whether it was because he was much older, or because she was just ready to move on and the jolt of sexual awareness she felt with Vishnu was just the thing she needed to face it, she had to make a decision.

This was, however, not the only interesting phone call she received that day. Simran had called her up in the morning and asked her to get in touch with Uday Pratap Singh, a young up-and-coming leader of the National Resurgence Party who had been running a crusade against corruption in the coalition government at the Centre. While he was not the tallest leader in the party, he was one of the more important ones, and, if the NRP came to power, he would be a cabinet minister, even though he was barely forty-one.

'Hello, may I speak to Uday Pratapji,' asked Janaki politely. 'I'm Janaki Rao from the *Indian Mail*.'

'Speaking,' came the deep voice at the other end.

Janaki plunged in. 'Oh, hello sir. I was asked to speak to you by my bureau chief Simran Kher. I believe there is something you wanted to talk about?'

'Yes, there is,' he said. 'Is it possible for you to come over to my residential office at 11 Bhagat Singh Marg at say 3 p.m.?'

'Yes sir,' she replied and hung up the phone. Uday Pratap Singh hailed from a minor political dynasty from the north Indian state of Uttar Pradesh, and was quite a pin-up, especially since Indian politicians were hardly a delight to the eyes. But the tall, slim, moustachioed Singh, with very light, brown-green eyes, had his share of female followers.

As she entered the office, she joined Simran, Monika and Shakira for their weekly powwow on the news priorities for the week.

'Rumour has it that Ilyas Khan will be rejoining the Janata Socialists yet again,' said Shakira, as Janaki wondered yet again at how the hip Shakira gelled with the old socialists of India's third front parties. The crusty old men in their dhotis seemed to have little in common with the trendy Shakira, who was groomed to within an inch of her life.

'It's the shock of the contrast, my dear,' Simran had said to her one day when Janaki had asked her. 'They just don't know how to play her; she's completely out of their league,' she added with a chortle. 'Imagine Satyaprakash Yadav confronted by Shakira's pathetic Hindi accent; he would answer just out of shock,' she said wiping away tears of mirth. Janaki was convinced that Simran had handed the Socialist parties over to Shakira just for the comic relief.

As the meeting ended, Simran asked Janaki about Uday Pratap Singh. 'Oh yeah, he's called me to his house at 3 p.m.,' said Janaki. Simran nodded and said something that pricked Janaki's ears to attention. 'Good. After you come back, the editor, you and I will have a meeting, so come straight back. We'll use agency copy if you miss anything.'

'Okay,' said Janaki. 'What is this about?'

'Just something we want to keep quiet about,' Simran answered. And Janaki had to be satisfied with that.

~

Janaki stared hard at a group picture of members of the sixteenth Lok Sabha, which occupied pride of place at Uday Pratap's office. His beaming bearded face looked back at her—he was thirty-seven in that picture, the first time he become an MP. He'd had a long stint in state politics, looking after the youth wing among other things.

'Aap andar chale jaiye, he will meet you now,' said Singh's secretary. Janaki walked in, automatically fishing out her notebook, pen and business card.

'Hello sir,' she said and handed him her card.

'Come in, come in,' said Singh, playing with a gorgeous golden retriever who lolled about at his feet. Janaki quickly noticed family pictures on the walls, including two very small boys. As she settled down, Singh noticed that she was looking at the pictures.

'Those are my sons, Siddhartha and Jaideep,' he said with a smile. 'They live in Lucknow.'

'They're very sweet,' Janaki said.

He smiled and asked her if she wanted some tea. As they settled down, he looked deep into her eyes, and said, 'Janaki, just put that notebook away. I called you here because I met Simran and Kishoreda at a dinner last night, and there is something that needs to be made public about which I need to put my cards on the table.' He fished out a set of documents from a file placed on the coffee table. 'Here, take a look at this. If you have any questions, after that we'll go over them.'

Taking the sheaf of papers from him, Janaki made out a few bank statements and some papers relating to the ownership details of strange companies. 'Er . . . sir, what are these papers? I really don't get it.'

'Let me explain this to you. Do you know the commerce minister D. Purushottamam?' he said. Janaki got a jolt. She said that she had interviewed him once. 'Well, his brother Shanmugham is one of the biggest arms dealers around, and is closing a deal for the acquisition of some $2.6 billion worth of aircraft for the Indian Air Force.'

'The papers I have given you relate to some shell companies he has set up, their bank transactions and also his front business of import and export,' said Singh. Janaki was a little taken aback. She was a political journalist, not an investigative one. Put her in an election she would come up trumps, but this was a little beyond her.

'I have wanted to give these papers to someone for a long time. I have done some work on this; I need you and the *Indian Mail* to check it out,' he said, tapping into her uncertainty. 'Look, I have this information; I'm passing it on. The news decision is for you to take. This is going to be one of the biggest scams to hit the country; the scale of the kickbacks on this deal is phenomenal.'

'But, sir, what does Purushottamam have to do with his brother's business?'

Singh almost smirked at her. 'I can't believe you have been a journalist for—how many years is it?'

'Six years, sir.'

'Yeah, six years and you don't know how influence is peddled in this town?'

Janaki felt like a naïve fool, but then she had asked a rather obvious question. 'I guess you are right,' she muttered.

'Please don't feel that you should be a natural-born cynic,' Singh said to her reassuringly. 'I have been in politics too long and dealt with too many of your tribe who are also cynics. 'I'm sorry,' he added for good measure.

'No, no, it's all right. If I'm naive, then I need to be told all these things.'

Singh stared at her long and hard. 'Janaki, we have to expose this. I know that a lot of people think that politicians and corruption go hand in hand, but this is to do with the defence of the country. I'm not cynical about that!'

Janaki nodded and took the papers. 'I'll call you once I figure this out.'

'No. I'll call you. I suspect my phones are tapped,' he said with a grin.

'I really don't know how you get any work done!' Janaki exclaimed involuntarily and almost bit her tongue. He smiled and shrugged. 'I believe that we are living in a post-privacy society; I assume that everything I do is open to scrutiny. Once you do that, it's normal.'

'Amazing,' she said, gathering her papers. 'It was nice meeting you, sir. I think you've said all that needs to be said.' As she was being ushered out of the house she saw a camera team from YTV, a news channel, parking their car. Janaki greeted Mrityunjay, the NRP reporter. 'Kya chal raha hai?' he asked.

Janaki immediately improvised. 'Sandeep Kumar, our opinion editor, wanted a piece from Uday Pratap for the edit page; just came to take that down,' she said and hustled out of the place.

When she got back to the office, Simran was waiting for her. 'You got the papers?' she asked. As Janaki nodded, Simran herded her to Kishoreda's cabin, where they were joined by Deepak Sharma.

Kishoreda went through the documents. 'See here, Apex Imports, owned by Shanmugham; other shareholders include Aruna, his wife, and P. Vidyaa, Purushottamam's wife. Janaki, we want you to do this story because you have some experience covering business as well. I want you to crosscheck all these papers, and not just the shareholding pattern of Apex Imports. Get on to the Registrar of Companies (RoC) website, find out who owns what, crosscheck this balance sheet of the last five years and track any anomalies and any Enforcement Directorate or tax notices. Take Deepak's help if you don't know how to go about it, and for heaven's sake, keep it under your hat!'

Janaki bobbed her head in agreement, but couldn't resist asking, 'Sir, is it correct for us to accept these papers from a member of the opposition? We know they are trying to trap the government; should we play into that?'

Kishoreda stared at her over his spectacles. 'Janaki, whenever some scam breaks or the truth comes out about a deal, it's always because an interested party passes on some information. Our job is to weigh whether this information coming out will serve the interests of the readers and whether the information is correct. Where it comes from is secondary. We are going to check this information out; if it's correct we will run the story. Does that answer your question?'

Janaki gulped and nodded.

'Remember, the story will always be sourced from an aggrieved party, but that does not mean it doesn't deserve to be out there. If money is being made on defence deals and these documents check out, we have a duty to put this out in public,' he said, dismissing them.

Janaki quietly filed out after Simran, still a little doubtful of her ability to deliver this. As soon as she went back to her desk she saw three missed calls, all from Vishnu. Strangely, it just reminded her that she was about to go out with a man who worked for someone she was about to do a demolition job on. She wondered whether she should tell Simran about her date and decided not to. I'll deal with this later, she thought to herself.

At around 7.30 p.m., early for her, Janaki slipped into the office loo. Taking out her tiny make-up kit, and a fresh top to wear over her pants, she quickly did her face. The jewel-toned maroon top was one of her favourites, and she always felt confident when she wore it. With one last spritz of her perfume, she tried to sidle out of the building hoping nobody would notice.

'Arrey, tu ladki ban kar kahan jaa rahi hai?' came a loud voice.

Damn and blast; of all the people—Jaiveer Singh, she said to herself. 'Shut up and get back to work, forests are depleting as you speak,' she replied (Jaiveer was their environment correspondent). Janaki's regular look was what she described as 'no-go chic', which was basically the 'no time for grooming look', with comfortable shoes.

Jaiveer grinned and ducked back behind his workstation. 'Hamara environment toh tumne chamka diya!' he said. Thankfully nobody bothered her after that, and Janaki eased into the car, ready to do battle with Delhi traffic.

The Leaping Frog had good music, even for a Monday evening, and lots of tables free. As Janaki walked in, she realized she was early and asked for a table at the far corner. As she settled down in her seat, she fished out her phone and texted Vishnu that she was already there.

'stck in trf' came the succinct reply.

What the hell, let me order my beer, she thought.

Vishnu stood at the entrance of the Leaping Frog and looked at Janaki, who was busy sipping beer and tucking into what looked like a steaming heap of tacos and cheese. He just grinned to himself at that, he could not have picked a woman who was more completely not his type even if he had gone looking for one.

'Do go on; you look like you are doing fine by yourself,' he said as he slid into the seat opposite her.

Janaki choked on a mouthful of taco and had to be slapped on the back to get back to normal. 'Hey! I was hungry! I'm coming straight from work,' she said.

He smiled and flicked a little bit of taco hanging from the side of her mouth. 'I'm sorry I was late, I just stopped at home for a shower.' His eyes slid hungrily over her: the top of her head, her high breasts but, most of all, those piercing eyes that looked directly into his.

'Umm . . . so what was your day like?' he asked, after placing their orders for drinks and starters.

Janaki felt a tiny twinge of guilt over the story she would have to pursue now. 'Er, just generally, hung around at the party office— they have a party executive meeting coming up, so there were stories and stuff. By the way, if you don't mind my asking, who was that woman with you last week?'

Vishnu put his stein of beer very carefully back on the table before answering. 'That was the woman I wanted to marry ten years ago.'

'Oh,' said Janaki, and cursed herself for asking the question. Lurid images of Vishnu and the mysterious woman in all sorts of positions chased each other in her mind.

'She is also posted here now and wanted to catch up, so it wouldn't be awkward when we bump into each other later.'

'Actually, that is a good idea. She is very beautiful.' And I'm soooo not your type, she added to herself.

'Yes, she is. Tell me, what is your physical type in a guy?' he asked suddenly. Janaki was floored by the question, not expecting this guerrilla attack.

'Umm, never thought of that. I started going out with Saurabh in college, and before that there were just some guys I used to hang out with, you know.'

'Hmmm . . .'

'Look, I kissed you because I am attracted to you, but I'm not going to sleep with you, okay?'

'Er . . . I don't recall anyone asking you to, girl!' he said with a grin.

Janaki grinned back sheepishly. 'Yeah, you're right, what I meant to say was that what I did in Chennai, I usually don't do that at all.'

'Look, I get it. We have a connection. I *will* ask you for a kiss at the end of the evening, so think about it in the meantime.' With that he asked for more drinks, leaving Janaki swinging between surprise and, she had to admit, happy anticipation.

'Speaking of physical types, I am nothing like that woman last week,' she said, determined to get more out of him on that subject.

'Hmmm . . .' he said, looking intently at her. And suddenly, just like that, he wanted to get out of the place where he could just kiss the hell out of this woman. 'Are you done?' he asked urgently.

'Er . . . yes, I guess,' she said, although she was still a little hungry.

'Okay, now, here is what we'll do. I'm driving myself; we will get out of this place, drive around for some time, find a place where I can kiss you and then drop you here so you can pick up your car,' he said signalling the waiter for the bill. Janaki should have objected to his high-handed manner, but she just nodded meekly, holding his gaze as his eyes moved over her face with unmistakable intent.

As they walked to his car, he held her hand possessively, only letting go once he reached it. As they both settled into their seats, a thought struck Janaki. 'Just where are we going to go? Towards Noida?'

'No way. With crime being the way it is, if we pull over anywhere, you'll be raped and I'll be buggered before we know it. We'll figure something out.'

They got out of Khan Market and made their way to central Delhi. The whole time, Vishnu did not let go of her hand; he kissed it and held it—even changing gears with it. Janaki just looked at him in wonder, a little shy at this display of aggression.

They drove around for a while before it struck Janaki that the VIP areas in Delhi were too well protected. 'Bloody hell, you never meet a cop when you are stuck in a jam, and here they are all over the place, with street lights blazing,' she muttered to herself.

Vishnu barked with laughter, and gave her a roguish look. 'We will persevere.'

Somewhere among the various Margs and bylanes, Vishnu finally stopped, took off his seat belt and jerked hers off, before hauling her to him for a deep kiss. Janaki couldn't help but be intensely aware that anybody could turn up and disturb them. Strangely, both of them kept their eyes open through the kiss. 'We are hopeless,' he said collapsing with laughter. 'We're both so cautious we'll never manage to neck in public!'

Janaki smiled, and, to make matters worse, her stomach decided to rumble at that very moment.

'Awww, you are hungry!' he said. 'Why didn't you tell me you wanted to eat something back at the restaurant?'

'Did you give me an opportunity?'

He smiled and settled back in the driver's seat. 'Let's go to Moolchand and have some parathas, what do you say?'

She grinned back at him, and teased, 'So, did your lady love's stomach ever growl in the middle of a kiss?'

He smiled. 'Nope, it sang a symphony! Come on now, that was ten years ago, and she would never have consented to parathas at a roadside stall either.'

They drove towards south Delhi and parked near one of the stalls making parathas. Only genuine Delhiites knew that this was one place in the city where you could get food in the middle of the night. They got out of the car and ordered what they wanted to eat. Vishnu turned around, clasped her waist and hoisted her on the bonnet of the car, where they spread their feast and gorged.

'Actually, I was hungry too,' he said, munching on the parathas.

Janaki nodded, saying, 'Don't distract me, I need food!' as she helped herself to some food off Vishnu's plate as well. Vishnu smiled back at her. He felt good here, now, with this girl who seemed unaware that butter was dribbling down her chin. Staring intently at her mouth, he ran a finger on her chin, taking the butter off and licking it off his own finger. As suddenly as that, the mood between them shifted.

'Janaki, I want you. We are not kids; how are we going to play this?'

'Vishnu, I really don't know. We can't meet at my place; it's a small housing society where all the aunties know me. It will be very awkward.'

'And I live with my mother,' he said with a heavy sigh.

She laughed out loud at that, and quickly shut her mouth at his frown.

'Why, what's wrong with that? I can hardly throw my mother out of her home, just because I've moved to Delhi!'

'No, no; I just remembered a joke about how Jesus was really an Indian man.'

'Why?' he asked, almost afraid to know the answer.

'Well, he lived with his mum till he was thirty-two; he thought she was a virgin and she thought he was god—that's your average relationship between an Indian mother and her son!'

He cracked a smile at that and said, 'Ah, yes, families: ties that bind and gag.'

She realized that she may have touched a raw nerve. 'Hey, it's an old joke, I didn't mean anything by it.'

'No, no; it's all right.'

Janaki still felt a little uncomfortable for having pissed him off. Visions flashed through her mind of them in bed with him staring stonily at her because she'd cracked an inappropriate joke at a crucial moment.

As if he could read her mind, Vishnu asked her, 'Er, are you much of a talker in bed?'

Janaki looked straight at him, poker-faced. 'You have to hear my in-bed comedy routine: laugh while you come, two-in-one service,' she said with a smart salute. He just stared at her as if she had grown horns. 'Relax, I'm sure you'll find a way to get me to shut up,' she said teasingly.

He smiled at that, but it was diffident. He liked to be the funny one, and this girl had a mouth on her that could be a problem.

'So, I'm assuming from all these discussions that you are formally asking me to sleep with you, Mr Singh?' she said to lighten the mood, and to make him feel less like he was with a troll.

He laughed and replied, 'I am asking you to make love with me, Ms Rao, and then, yes, eventually sleep. I hope you don't kick in your sleep or snore.'

'I think we are getting ahead of ourselves here; let's figure out a place first!'

Vishnu grinned. He knew he ought to be shocked at this easy contemplation of sex, but he felt relaxed and knew in his gut that sex with her would be full of laughs—something he hadn't known in a while. Even if her sense of humour was seriously scary.

~

The next morning Janaki lay in bed wondering just how her life had begun to go off the rails so fast. Here she was, about to end a six-year-long relationship and contemplating a new one while on the trail of a story which could shake things up in the establishment. Completely out of her depth in every way.

Sighing and flopping around on her bed, Janaki realized that she had to tell Saurabh that it was over. But there had been no fights, no showdowns, just a dying of feelings, she thought, so how does one initiate such a conversation?

As she let Jyotsna, her maid, in and gave her instructions for the cleaning routine, she dialled Saurabh's number.

'Hi,' said a sleepy voice at the other end. 'Sweets, how are you?'

As she started to speak she realized that somehow, whenever she called Saurabh, he always sounded sleepy. She brushed the thought aside and said, 'Saurabh, listen, we have to talk. Can you come over for breakfast or coffee or something so I can talk to you alone?'

'Why? What have I done now?'

Janaki immediately felt a frisson of irritation at that; again, the feeling that Saurabh had cast her in the role of a mother flashed through her.

'Can you just come here?'

'Haan, theek hai, eleven o'clock suit you?'

'Hmm, fine.'

Janaki was distracted the rest of the morning, filled with a strange feeling of apprehension. She and Saurabh had had more than their share of fights—rousing brawls where things were thrown—but they had always believed that they were in it for the long haul. This was something different. It's like saying goodbye to all my youthful illusions, she thought to herself.

At around 11.15 the doorbell rang and Janaki hurried to answer it. Saurabh stood outside leaning against the wall with a sheepish grin and an apology on his lips. 'I'm sorry, yaar, about Saturday, and for being late today.'

Janaki looked at him and was flooded with misgivings. This is Saurabh; I grew up with him! How can I do this? she thought. And she wondered, not for the first time, whether she would have broken up with him had she not met Vishnu.

'Come in,' she said without commenting on his apology. She went to the kitchen to make some coffee, and Saurabh followed her. As she leaned over the stove to put the pan on it, he wrapped his arms around her from behind.

'Hey, I said I'm sorry.'

'It's all right, Saurabh; I really don't care. I haven't for some time,' she said with a sigh.

'Oh god! Are we going to debate every little thing again? I said I'm sorry!'

'Saurabh, we are not going to debate anything,' she said, now feeling a little pissed off. 'We're done.'

'Oh, we're done, are we? Fine! I'm off! Call me when this snit you've got into is sorted out,' he said and made for the door.

'Wait. I won't be calling you; not to continue this Saurabh: we are done. I don't want to be with you any more.'

He just turned around and shook his head. 'You know, you've done this so many times, just raise your hand when you really mean it.'

Janaki slowly raised her hand and gazed steadily back at him. Saurabh just stared at her, confusion and disbelief chasing each other across his face. 'You don't mean that. Take it back!'

'It's over.'

'Who is he?'

Janaki flinched. This was where she was vulnerable, her moral high ground crumbling like a sandcastle in the wind.

'No one,' she lied.

'Come on! You don't expect me to believe that you aren't dumping me for someone else! Why else would you get pissed off over something that happens all the time?'

'Saurabh, maybe I am tired of your behaviour and just don't want to be around you any more!'

'I don't buy it. And don't try to give me this holier than thou shit; there is some other guy and, believe me, I'm going to find out who he is!'

'Look, I'm not arguing with you; I think it's enough that one of us thinks it's over. You told me that was all that was ever needed to end a relationship.'

'Oh, so now I'm someone you like to quote back, is it?' he asked sarcastically. 'God, Janaki! You treated like me like a barely tolerated kid and now I'm a savant at break-ups? Why don't you throw me those other disgusting clichés like "it's not you, it's me" or, better yet, "I think we've grown apart"?' he asked with a jibe in his voice.

Janaki winced because, frankly, those very words were waiting to trip out of her mouth. 'Saurabh, it's over. Truly,' she repeated helplessly, hoping that this scene would be over soon.

'So you called me over to your house, where the walls are so thin that the neighbours can hear you toss in your bed, to give me my marching orders? So I can't rail and rant at you? I expected more class, but then why did I? Fuck it. I'm done too; you can go to whoever is waiting in the wings. Better luck to that poor sod.'

As he was walking out of her apartment, Saurabh turned back. Janaki just stared at him. He walked up to her and mumbled, 'I want my iPod back.'

Janaki just raised an eyebrow, walked to her handbag and fished the iPod out.

'Here.'

Saurabh silently took it from her and walked out.

Janaki looked at her watch; the time was 12.10. She felt like a heel, because she knew that Saurabh was right. If Vishnu had not been around she probably would not have broken up with him. So what does that make me? she wondered.

~

As she walked into the NRP headquarters at Rajaji Marg, Janaki met up with her 'beat gang'—a group of reporters who, like her, covered the NRP and hung around together. Shilpa Jha and Vinay Sharma, her closest friends on the beat, were waiting for her near the office canteen sipping tea.

'Hi,' Janaki said, a little low on the pep quotient. 'Kya chal raha hai?'

'Nothing yaar, Rajiv Singh is going to brief us on this Kashmir bust-up at 1 p.m.,' Vinay said.

Shilpa looked at her and frowned. 'Umm, Janaki, what happened?' she asked in a whisper.

Janaki couldn't prevent a little tear from rolling down her cheek. 'Saurabh and I broke up this morning.'

'Oh Janaki, why?'

'Well, I initiated it but now I feel like such a heel!'

'Par kya hua?'

Janaki didn't want to share all the details with Shilpa. They were close, but in a professional sort of way; for her personal confessionals she still depended on her best friend Kajal. Kajal and she hadn't spoken in weeks, thanks to Kajal's high-profile job as a buyer for a major international fashion house—it involved a lot of travel.

'Nothing, it was just time,' Janaki said, and walked into the briefing room, making it quite clear that she didn't want to discuss it. She called Kajal, suddenly quite desperate to talk to her friend and sounding board. She got her voicemail and decided to leave a message. 'Hi Kaj, Janaki here. Call me; I need to talk,' she said into her phone and cut the call.

As she walked into the briefing room, she was taken aback to see Uday Pratap holding court with a group of television journalists near the podium. He looked at Janaki and then appeared to look right through her after a brief nod. Janaki nodded too and joined the crowd around Rajiv Singh, the official spokesperson, who quickly briefed them on the increasingly confusing Kashmir talks.

Janaki had tuned out by the end—Vishnu and Saurabh, not to mention the entirely new investigative reporting aspect of her job, were putting her off her feed. Just then her phone rang. It was Kajal.

'Hey, what happened?'

'Oh Kaj, are you free this evening? Can you come over, please, I really need you!'

'Of course! What happened? Don't scare me, yaar!'

'I broke up with Saurabh, for good this time. I need you.'

Kajal sighed at the other end. 'Sure, I will be there. What's your poison?'

'Umm, how about a nice bottle of wine?' Kajal was quite proud of her collection of wine, and they frequently met up for an epicurean feast.

Janaki felt immeasurably better after that, and even managed to put all her worries behind her. As she dragged herself to office that evening, Simran was waiting for her with a sheaf of papers. 'This next set has to be verified, Janaki,' she said. Janaki took the papers and walked into the tiny conference room to go over them with Deepak.

They were company balance sheets for the last five years. Janaki was no expert but her training in accounts in school came in handy, helping her get to the heart of the matter. 'What the hell, they're not striking huge deals but are just afloat! Look at the payments for small services that they're providing for this Hillgate Trust, and this other trust, Rothman's!'

Simran looked up with a twinkle in her eye. 'That's exactly it, Janaki! These trusts have connections we need to probe.' The trusts had offices in London; that kind of stumped them a little. 'We need to source this properly; you may have to travel there,' said Simran.

Janaki decided that since she was in the line of fire, she would do this her way. 'Simran, you have to hand these papers over to me. I need to go through these balance sheets and the details of these eight bank accounts. I'll do some digging and get back to you. I think the RoC website is going to be my best friend for some time!'

Simran raised an eyebrow at that. 'Simran, you asked me to do this, let me do it my way.'

The one bright spot with this story was the fact that Janaki got to go home early that night. She stopped on the way and bought some cheese and crackers, and some sinful chocolate cake. I refuse to go through a break-up without chocolate, she said to herself, as she let herself into the house.

She had barely put her purchases down when her phone rang. It was her mother. 'Hello Amma.'

'Janaki, what is this I'm hearing? You've broken up with Saurabh? The poor boy called me up in quite a state!'

Janaki's mouth fell open. Saurabh had always avoided her family or, as he put it, 'family scenes' in all their years together. The only time he spoke to Mythili Rao, Janaki's mother, was on her birthday or his, when she called up. Janaki's mother was fond of him though and felt he was a 'nice boy'.

'Amma, I have very good reasons for what I'm doing. I can't believe he called you! Even I didn't call you!' she wailed.

'I know; why didn't you, kanni?'

'Amma, I will deal with it; I'll be okay, please! Kajal is coming over now, so I'll be fine.'

Mythili Rao sighed on the phone, and said, 'Just be very sure about what you are doing, love; sometimes you hit difficult patches, then they go away.'

'Yeah, I know, but I'm very sure, Amma.'

As her mother hung up the phone, Janaki found herself wracked by doubt again. How could I break up with Saurabh, she wondered again.

'Very easily,' said Kajal, an hour later, as they settled on Janaki's bed with a glass of wine each. 'You know that this was going nowhere for some time, yaar; you know that we were all good friends in college, and it seemed like you and Saurabh always had it together, but over the last couple of years, it looks like he's made up his mind to be the infant in the relationship. What was all that nonsense about being a struggling artist while you picked up the pieces? If he was so moved by his passion for films, why didn't he move to Mumbai and struggle like Mukul; why pitch for these safe government-sponsored documentaries?'

All of which sounded reasonable to Janaki.

'For heaven's sake, Janaki, you have moved your life around Saurabh for six years, and he has been shamelessly taking advantage of it! You need to strike out!'

As they talked through the night, Janaki realized that even if she did get involved with Vishnu, she would not allow another man to 'run her' like Saurabh had managed to do.

'No man will say no if you offer him everything on a platter. You need to keep something back for yourself,' Kajal said.

'You're right,' said Janaki, now quite determined to stand her ground. Just then her phone rang. Janaki expected to see Vishnu's number flashing—he had gone to Madurai with Purushottamam for the inauguration of a flyover there—but it was a private number. Curious, she answered the phone and was surprised by the voice on the other end.

'Hello.' It was Uday Pratap, his deep baritone coming down the phone line sending a shiver down Janaki's back.

'Oh, hello sir.'

'Janaki, I called to tell you that, while you are a good reporter, there is so much more you can do with your life, you know.'

Janaki raised her brows in surprise; she wanted to ask him if he had perhaps had a little too much to drink.

'Er, thank you sir. What do you suggest?' she asked, pulling a face at Kajal and shrugging her shoulders.

'You should join politics! Chalo, main tumhe NRP se ticket dilwa deta hoon.'

Janaki burst out laughing. 'Really? You would do that?

'Yes, chehra dekh kar to ek baar log elect kar hi lenge,' he said teasingly. Janaki was a little taken aback. 'I hope you don't mind my saying it, but I think you are very beautiful.'

'Thank you sir, but quite unnecessary I think.'

'Nonsense, beautiful women should always be told they are beautiful. Anyway, I think I have shocked you enough, have a good night.'

'Good night,' Janaki replied and disconnected the call.

Janaki turned to Kajal and let out her breath with a whoosh. 'Now what was that?' she exclaimed.

'Yeah, what was that?' asked Kajal.

'I don't know, I meet this guy for a story, he is very businesslike, and now suddenly he calls me out of the blue!'

'Seems he has a little crush on you,' Kajal said teasingly.

'I don't know. I'm doing something important for him, maybe he's just trying to sweeten me up.'

Kajal had been told about Janaki's assignment. 'Listen, he already has your bosses on board, he doesn't have to bother about that with you. Anyway, he is hot, let's grant him that!'

Janaki nodded in agreement and wondered at herself again.

First, one boyfriend for six years, then suddenly two guys out of the blue, she thought to herself. Just what the hell is happening?

~

The next morning, as Janaki battled a hangover, she checked her phone. There were three messages: an exhortation to buy cheap real estate at easy credit, and a message each from the two men now beginning to occupy her thoughts quite badly. Vishnu informed her that he had returned from Madurai, while Uday Pratap's message was more intriguing. 'Had to tell you that I couldn't take my eyes off you yesterday . . .'

Ooops, thought Janaki, and immediately felt irritated with herself. What the hell are you up to, girl? Barely through one break-up, poised to get into another relationship and happy that a third man finds you hot? she thought to herself. Recklessly abandoning all these cautioning voices, she replied: 'tks . . . never realized that you were staring.'

The reply was immediate: 'credit me with some technique, girl!'

At this Janaki sent back a smiley and quite determinedly put it out of her mind. Today she would be tracking the RoC, and finding out the ownership details of Apex Imports. She reached office early—because newspaper offices were quite deserted in the mornings, the trick, when writing difficult copy, was to reach early and work in silence. Janaki switched on her computer and started trawling through the RoC website; she had an account there because of her previous beat covering companies and corporates. What the site revealed was, to put it mildly, rather worrying. All the information Uday Pratap had given them checked out. Both the shareholding pattern and the balance sheets, which Janaki went through with a fine-toothed comb, matched his information.

What was also strange was an income tax notice the company had received a couple of months ago, asking for an explanation of some discrepancy between assets and their value. It was a good morning's work, but it filled Janaki with foreboding; it was clear she was getting into deep waters. Nothing in her short and protected life as the daughter of university professors living in a campus had prepared her for this. She was going to take on some powerful people, and she just could not shake off the misgivings she had over the source of the papers. It seemed like a political war, and she didn't want to be used in the bargain, knowing with some certainty that she would end up paying the heaviest price for it. We'll cross that bridge when we get to it, she said to herself, and decided that she had justified her salary for the day.

It was clear that, despite not getting export orders, Apex had a fairly good sum of money, accruing, very strangely, from a couple of service contracts with two UK-based trusts. Why would anyone pay three times the amount for these services, thought Janaki to herself.

As she was getting out of the building, she got an SMS alert. Checking her phone, she saw a message from Uday Pratap: 'cld u suggest a good site to download music from?'

'try YouTube or tinyurl?' she replied. She wasn't very tech-savvy, but this even she knew. 'tks' came the reply. Janaki raised her eyebrows at that, and walked on. Vishnu's office was close by and she contemplated dropping in; she wanted to see him quite badly. She hadn't seen him in a couple of days and so much had happened.

'Hi,' she said breathlessly on the phone. 'I'm nearby, can I drop in?'

'Er, not really. We have to catch up on quite a bit of work here. I'll call you in a while?'

Janaki was a little taken aback by his answer, for she had been quite longing to see him again, and maybe steal a kiss, but Vishnu's cold reaction pissed her off a little.

'Okay,' she said, a little shortly, and hung up the phone.

Vishnu looked at the phone and guessed that Janaki was a little put off by his tone, but he was determined to pace this out properly. He wanted her, but everything would run according to his pace, he had decided. No puppy love business, he said to himself.

Janaki stalked off, a little upset with it all, and saw that her phone was ringing again.

It was Uday Pratap again. 'Hi, are you around Claridges?'

'Yeah, I guess.'

'Would you like to have a cup of coffee at Pickwicks?'

'Er, sure,' she said, genuinely surprised that this was happening.

She pulled into Claridges, handed her keys over to the valet parking attendant, and went in, hoping her hair looked okay. She entered the tiny, sunny restaurant and saw Uday Pratap, dressed in trousers and shirt—a very un-neta-like outfit—reading a newspaper.

He rose when she arrived to take her seat. 'Thank you for joining me,' he said.

She waved off his words saying, 'No, no, I was not busy.'

'Janaki, I wanted to apologize for that day, I think I offended you.'

'Not really, you are more experienced about the world.'

Smiling, he said, 'All the more reason I should have been a little gentler.'

'Sir, I know enough of the world to know that you haven't called me here to apologize to me,' she said, suddenly curious as to why he had called her over.

A little taken aback at her direct speech, he responded, 'Er, about last night, I hope you didn't take that amiss, I don't do this as a habit.'

'Sir, I know you don't, and I figured that you were at a very happy place,' she said with a smile.

He laughed out loud. 'You could say that. It's a rare pleasure to get an evening to myself, so I must have said some stuff that might have seemed odd to you.'

She nodded and grinned. 'Yeah, it seemed like that to me.'

He looked at her with narrowed eyes, his gaze alighting on her features one by one, and Janaki couldn't help but feel a tingle at every place it touched.

Oh good god, what is wrong with you, she said to herself. You are already into someone else; how can this be happening?

'So, what kind of coffee do you like? Cappuccino?' he asked breaking the tension.

'Yes,' she said. He ordered their coffee, asking for a double espresso.

'So, what do you do when you are not chasing stories?'

Now Janaki felt she had a choice. She could string this along and be polite, or she could just do what she was good at and ask some straight questions. 'I wonder why a handsome neta calls me up late in the night,' she said saucily.

He smiled back at her and said, 'You won't let that go, will you.'

'Nope. Not for a bit.'

Taking a deep breath, he said, 'That day, when you came into my office, I didn't expect you to be so young and, frankly, so lovely. Look, I'm not saying anything except that it was one of those one-off things that happened; please don't be offended,' he said sipping his coffee.

'Sir . . .' she started.

'Please call me Uday.'

'Look, I can't do that. You are a professional acquaintance and much older. I don't mind the fact that you called me, or that you said all those things. It was okay as a one-off thing, but we both know it was inappropriate.'

'It won't happen again, Janaki, I'm really sorry.'

They continued to talk of inconsequential things, discovering a shared love of Pablo Neruda. 'Tonight I can write the saddest lines,' they said together as if on cue.

'Well, I'm glad your education was not neglected. Nowadays I find that I can't understand any version of Hindi or English spoken by young people!'

'Oops, and you are a *yuva* neta!'

He laughed out loud. 'My dear girl, I'm glad that I'm in politics, because even at forty-one I can parade as a youth leader.' They both smiled and, as he settled the bill, he suddenly stopped and said to her, 'By the way, what is the progress on the special project?'

'Continuing,' she said. 'Fingers crossed,' she added, unwilling to share any details. The criss-crossing of lines was making her uncomfortable, and, despite what Kishoreda said, she had issues with the sourcing of their tip-off.

Uday Pratap seemed to tap into that. As he gathered his things and got up to leave, he said to her, 'This is not a motivated thing, Janaki; it's a genuine scam.'

She nodded, and decided that nothing else needed to be said. She got up and, shaking hands with him, left.

As she exited the hotel, Janaki couldn't help but wonder whether she was being led up the garden path on this one. Kishoreda, you better be right, she muttered to herself. The flattery and the flirting were forgotten by the time she got back to office.

~

Vishnu stared at his phone, trying to decide whether to call Janaki or not. He knew she was a little miffed with him, but he wanted to be very clear on certain things. This relationship would run according to his rules or not at all. He didn't want to be in a position where he would have to choose, but, if push came to shove, he would make a choice.

Sighing, he called Janaki's number, expecting a cold reaction. 'Hi,' he said tentatively.

'Hi,' came the reply as chirpy as ever. 'You took your time calling,' she said teasingly.

He laughed. 'So you're not pissed off?' he asked, a little chagrined actually that she appeared unaffected.

'No, its okay. You were busy you said; what's there to take offence to?' Janaki almost bit her tongue when she said that, for she had been rather put off this afternoon. But further reflection and a brief powwow with Monika had convinced her that this was not the way to go.

'Take your time, Janaki, and for heaven's sake don't throw tantrums like a kid. Just be relaxed; this has to be totally different from the mother–son thing with Saurabh,' Monika had told her.

'So, would you like to meet up for dinner at some point during the week,' he asked, still puzzled.

'Actually, I'm off to Muzaffarpur tomorrow, and will be back only Friday night.'

'Why? What's going on there?'

'Nothing, just some stories on a spate of arrests from some madrasas there,' she said almost dismissively.

'Oh, okay. When can I see you then?'

'Sometime after Friday. I'll text you when I'm back.'

'Yeah, okay,' he said, his voice a little small now.

'Bye then,' she said cheerily, and hung up the phone. It had gone better than expected, she thought. Ha! Play games, will you? Play that! she said to herself.

Vishnu was, in fact, feeling a little bemused at the turn of the conversation. He had expected a little tantrum and then a gradual giving in; this cheerful casualness was a little pissing off. She'd said she would break up with the other guy; had she done that? he wondered.

All his intentions of playing it cool dissolved in a whirl of uncertainty. He called her back.

'Yes, hi.'

'I was wondering, did you break up with Saurabh or is that something I'm not supposed to ask about?'

'Of course you are entitled to ask. And yes, we did break up on Tuesday. I wanted to talk to you about that. Can we do that later? I'm a little rushed here.'

'Er, okay. Is that why you wanted to see me this afternoon? I had a lot on my plate, all right?' he said almost belligerently.

'Listen, all of us have work to do. It's all right. Was there anything else?'

'Um, no. See you next week then. Can I call when you are away?'

'Yes, of course.'

Now *that* is the way this is going to go, Mr Singh, she thought to herself as she hung up for the second time.

Her preoccupation with Vishnu was hardly comparable to her absolute terror at the story she was attempting to investigate. Not only would it put Purushottamam in the dock, she was also in the dark about how it would affect this thing between her and Vishnu.

And yet she wasn't very sure whether she wanted any of it to come out any time soon. Let the story break, she kept telling herself, like a talisman that would resolve all her conflicts.

Eight

As she got back into the city from a very disturbing trip to Muzaffarpur, Janaki sighed. She had had a series of meetings with the families of the boys arrested from several madrasas in the area. Intercepts by intelligence agencies had implicated those boys in a terror module. Like most things associated with questionable intelligence, the arrests were creating a controversy.

The situation made Janaki realize the limitations of her job. She could highlight the stories—some would say that was enough— but to walk away with just that and not have any real power to help always left her feeling a little frustrated. The one good thing about the trip was the fact that Vishnu had called her every one of those three days. They had had long rambling chats about all their jobs, lives, friends and things that should have been discussed over the course of several dates, but they did over the phone.

She found out that he could be a cussed pig about many things, something that worried her. She also realized that her tendency to give in was something she had to curb, otherwise it would be like Saurabh all over again. But most of all, Vishnu was too hung up on control, leaving her sick of being jerked around on a string.

At the end of it she also realized that he was part of the establishment and she was a reporter; they just didn't see most things the same way. But the attraction was still strong, and they kept returning to how they could just be together.

'Nothing to it; I'll fix something. You don't worry your head over it,' he said every time she raised her doubts over their relationship.

As she entered her house, Mrs Mishra, her neighbour, snoopy as they get, caught her. 'Beta, Saurabh had come looking for you, he said that he wanted you to call him,' she said, quite obviously curious that he had left a message with her and not called Janaki directly. Janaki was furious with Saurabh after that and told him so when she called him. 'Why are you doing this!' she almost screamed at him. 'You can call me, you know, why did you have to leave a message in such a melodramatic fashion!'

'I don't have to answer to you any more, Janaki. I want my stuff back, my books and CDs and some shirts I had left at your apartment. I just want to know when would be a good time to pick them up,' he replied nonchalantly, totally unfazed by her reaction.

'Saurabh, you can come any time; why are you behaving like this?'

'I'm out of your life now, Janaki, so I have to be formal.'

'Oh please, spare me the drama,' she interjected, quite exasperated now. 'I'll leave the keys with Javed. You can come in and take your things and get him to drop the keys at my office. Will that suit you?'

'Yeah, okay. I'll leave a list of things I have taken.'

'Yeah, whatever,' she said and hung up the phone.

~

The air was getting chillier in Delhi as Diwali edged closer and temperate winds replaced the hot blast of the easterlies. Janaki took a long hot bath and was towelling her hair when the phone rang. It was Uday Pratap.

'Where have you been?' he asked a little angrily.

'Muzaffarpur . . .' she responded, not understanding his anger.

'Can I talk to you?'

'Yes.'

'It's nothing; I just needed to know where I can buy a nice guitar.'

Janaki was a little taken aback. 'Er, yeah, I guess you could go to Daryaganj, there are some very good shops that stock instruments,' she said slowly, wondering where it was going. 'You thinking of learning?'

'No,' he sighed. 'It's for my son Siddhartha. I went to his parent–teacher meeting the other day and I didn't even know that he had been taking lessons in school. He seems a little angry at me, you know. He just dismissed me, saying "Aapko aur bhi bahut kuch nahin pata." I tell you I felt like a piece of shit.'

Janaki raised her eyebrows at that. Frankly, parenting and the maternal instinct were a little removed from her plans, so she really couldn't fathom why Uday Pratap wanted to talk to her about it.

'Yeah, that is a little disturbing. Why don't you move them to Delhi or wherever you live most?'

There was a short pause.

'You know, when I started out, Lucknow was where I spent most of my time. And then, my relatives are around all the time so I thought my wife would feel more secure there alone with the children. I didn't want to send them to boarding school because I missed my mother too much when I was sent to boarding school. But now I don't know what to do. Maybe I should move them to Delhi . . .' he said almost thinking aloud.

Janaki didn't know how to respond to that. 'I guess you could try. I don't know what your lifestyle is like, but why don't you ask your colleagues what their experience has been?'

'Yeah, I guess you are right.'

Janaki hung up the phone and wondered again why Uday Pratap had called her up in the first place. It seemed like too trivial an issue to discuss. The next minute all of it flew out of the window as she got a text message from Vishnu: 'A friend's place is available next Saturday; I have the keys.'

Janaki's heart started thudding. Was she ready for this? Hell, yes! She had wanted Vishnu from the day they met. She texted back 'free on Saturday but u'll have to pay for it thereafter! ;)'. He sent a smiley back.

～

At office the next day, Janaki went up to Simran's cabin and told her that she had unearthed some interesting details. 'Simran, there are offices of Apex imports and exports in the UK, housed in expensive properties near Hyde Park. I need to find out from the land registry office in London who paid for these properties. In the UK, fortunately, they have to declare the source of funds while registering property.'

Simran perked up. 'That's great work. Try and find out soon. In fact, we can sponsor a trip to London to do it. I'll get Kishoreda to clear it soon.'

Janaki nodded unenthusiastically.

'What happened, Janaki?'

Janaki sighed. 'It's the fact that we may be playing an unwitting pawn in somebody else's plans that bugs me.'

Simran looked at her and repeated something she had said often. 'Reporters are the infantry of the newspaper; we follow orders and go to the front when asked to.'

Janaki said nothing. Whenever she came up against an implacable opinion, she refused to argue, hoping time would prove her right. In her opinion, it was a waste of breath. For now she just wanted to focus on something frivolous, like what she would wear for her first time with Vishnu. She wanted to keep the entire thing under wraps, so she was pretty much on her own. She texted Vishnu: 'Is there something in particular you fancy me wearing?'

'How about some silver anklets . . . and nothing else,' came the prompt reply.

Janaki smiled, and then cursed herself. I had to ask!!! No money and no anklets; now I'm stuck, she thought.

After that train of thought reached a dead end, Janaki did the one thing guaranteed to get her out of any jam; she called her mother. 'Amma, I'm really stuck with this story. I've hit a dead end in fact.'

'What happened?'

'I need to find out something from London, and I don't know anyone there.'

'Arrey, Dave Uncle is there; he has retired from University, but he was down in Bangalore for the Indo–UK Conference just a month ago. Just mail him, kanni, I'm sure he'll know someone who can help you.'

If Janaki were able to send kisses through the phone her mother would have had a big one planted on her. Dave Houghton was an ex-armyman who had continued his education after he was demobbed. An acknowledged expert in South Asian studies, he was a long-time friend of both her parents, and still kept in touch with Mythili Rao.

'Amma, you are a genius! I really don't know what I would do without you!'

Mythili Rao just laughed. 'Are you sure you can't make it to Bangalore for Shruti's wedding?'

Shruti was Janaki's cousin, a lawyer trained at the National Law School. She had decided to marry her college sweetheart; the wedding was in a month.

'No, Amma, I can't get leave. Just send me Dave Uncle's email; I need to get on to this fast.'

'I'll do that. Are you okay though? I hope Saurabh has behaved like a gentleman.'

'Yes, Amma. You know him.'

'One never knows what strong emotions will set off, dear.'

'True,' Janaki said, frowning a little. Now that she thought about it, several of their common friends had stopped answering her calls, and she saw on her Facebook that they'd also had a party last week, to which she had not been invited and Saurabh certainly had.

'Amma, I have to go now.'

'Okay dear, call me on Sunday,' her mother replied and hung up.

While her mother had provided a direction for her to move her story, she had also given her food for thought as far as Saurabh was concerned. He had been very quiet, and the fact that many of their common friends had stopped answering her calls was worrying. Janaki decided to bite the bullet and called up Srividya in Chennai.

'Hi Sri,' she greeted her friend. 'Wassup?'

'Hiiii,' Sri replied. 'I was about to mail you. What's this I'm hearing, you and Saurabh broke up? Jai aur Veeru no more?'

Janaki smiled a little at that—she and Saurabh had been like a comedy tag team at most of their college dos and had been nicknamed Jai and Veeru, Salim and Javed and even Laxmikant–Pyarelal as a joke.

'Yeah, yeah. And no chance of a reunion concert either.'

Sri chuckled. 'He's been calling up and informing people, and, of course, gently interrogating us all on who his replacement is.'

Janaki winced. 'Sri,' she began, 'let him bitch about me, yaar, but I want to know why Shiv, Puneet and Ritu have stopped taking my calls.'

'They seem to have decided to go with him. Apparently break-ups mean dividing up friends as well.'

Despite her generally nonchalant attitude, Janaki was a little taken aback. 'You mean you guys got together and actually discussed this?' she asked, frankly a little disgusted now.

'Janaki, don't get upset. Saurabh has been beating the bush telegraph over it, and, frankly, no one saw this coming. You weren't talking to anyone, so everyone just got his version.'

'Well, hell, why am I surprised that Saurabh would rush to occupy the moral high ground?' Janaki replied, now roused to anger. 'And you guys decided to take sides, is it?'

Sri took a deep breath. 'Only those three, yaar. I didn't. I told him that both of you are my friends.'

'Whatever. What has to happen, will. But thanks for being a pal.'

'Sure,' her friend responded. They chatted about a bit more before she hung up the phone—quite deflated and upset. Dealing with a break-up while she was out of her depth professionally was getting her down. Before she could get on the self-pity express though, her phone beeped an SMS. Her mother had sent her Dave Houghton's email address. Oh, Amma to the rescue again, she thought. Despite the fact that she kept saying to herself that she didn't much care what her friends thought, and clichés like 'their loss, not mine', she knew she was pretty disturbed. Nothing like watching the world cast down from the moral high ground, she thought to herself.

Janaki logged on to her computer and sent off an email to Dave Houghton, mentioning both the trusts she wanted information about, the details of their properties in London and the details she required from the London land registry office.

Just as she finished, Shakira, blast her, sidled up to Janaki. 'Hey, what is this I'm hearing, yaar, you and Saurabh are no longer an item?'

For god's sake, Janaki thought, 'item'? Seriously, who got her a job in journalism? she added viciously to herself.

'We're no longer together, that's true,' she said evenly.

'Oh that's a shame, because I met him at the ICCR party for the music festival and he's such a cutie pie! What happened?' Shakira asked, puerile curiosity fairly oozing out of her.

Janaki gave her pained expression and said, 'Shakira, I don't really want to talk about it.' At that time Janaki came to a startling realization, that it had been easy dealing with Saurabh and telling him that their relationship was over; it was going to be much tougher to explain it to the world, which by god, wants its pound of flesh, she thought with a sense of resignation.

Over the years, especially when it came to her professional colleagues, Saurabh had been accepted as her boyfriend, invited to their parties and included in all gatherings. Therefore the news of the break-up had spread far and wide.

Note to self, with future relationships, no social outings till I'm very, very committed, she muttered to herself. Vishnu Singh, you will be a dark secret, she added for good measure. For all the purported liberal work atmosphere, journalists were, at a very basic level, suckers for rumour and gossip. Janaki felt the sting of being the target of it for the first time.

Ignoring Shakira and the rest of the bureau, Janaki turned back to her computer and started surfing the net to distract herself. Ten minutes of that and her phone beeped again. 'Want me to bring the anklets?' It was Vishnu.

Janaki smiled and instantly answered yes. In all the murkiness of gossip, she had forgotten that she was going to get naked in front of a strange man for the first time in six years. Sucking her tummy in, she did a mental review of her lingerie selection and clothes, and wondered whether to get a full wax. Now those are the things I should worry about, she thought to herself.

To distract herself, she made up a list of things she had to do before she could allow herself to be naked in front of Vishnu.

1. Full body deforestation and an oil massage.
2. Pick up new lingerie (will stretch credit, but what the hell).
3. Always remember, the left side is your best side.
4. Will get high before getting down 'n' dirty.
5. Eat but not pig before the deed.

She knew the last item would be a little difficult to manage since eating was a nervous reflex with her. Calling up her beauty parlour, she made the appointment for a full wax the next day and, casting her old friends to perdition, decided that work would be her life. Except, she had reached a dead end with her story. I can't catch a break, she said to herself rather miserably.

~

'Ow, what the bloody hell!' Janaki yelled as the dimunitive parlour assistant viciously pulled out a swathe of hair off her legs. 'Vishnu Sinha better give me bloody multiple orgasms for this,' she said to herself rather audibly.

'Didi, kya kaha?' the assistant asked, calmly inflicting what had to be at least second-degree torture.

'Kuch nahin!' Janaki replied curtly through clenched teeth. 'Can you get another person and finish this off quickly?'

The assistant shook her head. 'We don't have anyone free right now. Don't worry, I'll do it quickly.'

'Can't be quick enough for me!'

The assistant smiled and said, 'Didi, this is nothing, We have people who calmly go through Brazilian wax.'

'So give them a medal, yaar; no man is worth that much pain,' she snapped back. 'Er, what is a Brazilian wax?' she asked a little sheepishly.

'It's not for you, didi, aap rehne do,' the assistant replied. Janaki had to be satisfied with that.

It was two days to ground zero, as she referred to their planned meeting at one of Vishnu's college mate's flat. The friend had a business meeting out of town, and had taken his wife and children with him. 'The house will be ours during the day. I have to go back home in the evening,' Vishnu said.

Janaki retorted that she too had to be home early as she had some writing to finish on a special story.

She had gauged that Vishnu was a bit of a control freak, and that it could be a problem later. Not to mention all these things that I have to do to myself! she thought. With Saurabh, they had reached a stage where they barely noticed each other, never mind noticing body hair.

Janaki had not thought about sex much for a while, what with trying to break into political reporting and the everyday routine of her life with Saurabh. But connecting with Vishnu, and even, if she was honest with herself, Uday Pratap, had shown her how much she had missed it.

She had picked out some lingerie but felt so self-conscious about it that she kept looking at herself in the mirror. Bloody jiggly belly! Please god, no more samosas, please make this disappear, she wailed to herself. But that was, of course, not to be and she had to resign herself to making sure that Vishnu was not given too much of a view. Just how am I going to manage that? she thought to herself.

~

Across town, Vishnu was a little jittery. Not only was this going to happen on somebody else's turf, he also had to make sure Janaki felt comfortable about everything. He had the keys picked up from Ranbir Khanna's office in the afternoon. On a whim he had also bought chunky silver anklets for Janaki. Not too kinky I hope, he thought to himself.

He texted her. 'Any particular kind of wine?' 'Chardonnay' came the swift answer. He picked up the wine and some chocolates and put them in his car, in an ice box, so that his mother wouldn't wonder about them, and then almost cracked a grin at what Janaki would think of his precautions. Jesus Christ indeed, he chuckled to himself.

When he entered his house, he was in for a shock. Indira Singh, his mother, was sitting calmly sipping tea with Gayatri. He remembered that they'd met at a party and decided to go back to Vishnu's house after.

They looked up as Vishnu came in, and he was even more surprised to discern a shocking resemblance between his mother and the young woman. Good god, I had a lucky escape; thank you Pramod Dhar, he said in silent prayer to Gayatri's husband.

'Come, beta, Gayatri is here to see you. We've met up after such a long time, it was good to catch up,' said his mother. 'Both of you sit and chat, I'll tell Ramadin to get you more tea.'

'Er, hello Gayatri. I'm sorry but I just came in to take a shower. I'm on my way to an early dinner somewhere. I wish you'd called me and told me you were going to come over,' he said to her and saw, with disbelief, a crestfallen expression flash across her face.

'No, no, Vishnu, I just dropped by on a whim. You go ahead

with your plans. It was nice catching up with Aunty,' she said and rose to leave.

'Nonsense, beta, you must have one more cup of tea. Vishnu, you never told me you were going to be out for dinner. Never mind, have a cup of tea with Gayatri and then leave.' Not for the first time Vishnu wished that his father was alive; if anyone had the measure of Indira Singh, it was the late Pratap Singh.

Vishnu sat down on the sofa opposite Gayatri and wondered again whether he had fallen down a hole like Alice in Wonderland. This is something I would have given anything for ten years ago, he thought to himself.

Just then, Gayatri spoke up. 'Look, I didn't mean to intrude or anything. I just came to see you.'

'Yeah, yeah, it's fine,' he replied. He wanted to tell her that she was making him uncomfortable but then thought better of it.

'I . . . I don't know how to put this to you . . . when we met that day I said things which may have sounded different from the way I meant them,' Gayatri started.

'Look, Gayatri, I really didn't think much of anything. To tell you the truth, I was surprised that you got in touch in the first place,' he said, now quite eager for her to leave.

'But all the things that I said, and what we meant to each other . . .' she said and trailed off. Vishnu began to feel a little guilty, and then felt more of a heel as he saw tears well up in her eyes.

'Please, Gayatri, don't cry,' he said ineffectually. She sniffed a little, and very suddenly looked up at him and asked, 'Who is she, Vishnu?' That took him aback like nothing else.

'What? What did you say?'

'You have that look in your eyes, that distracted look. You're seeing someone, aren't you?'

Vishnu was saved from answering by Ramadin, who walked in with the tea. As they both sipped quietly, Vishnu marvelled at the vagaries of fate. This woman, ten years ago, would have had me over the moon with this possessiveness, he thought to himself.

As tea got over, Gayatri got up to leave. 'Vishnu, Pramod is going away on Saturday for a seminar to Bhubaneswar. Why don't you drop in for lunch?'

Vishnu almost agreed, but remembered in time that he would be meeting Janaki. 'I have other plans, Gayatri, maybe some other time.' She gave him a last reproachful look and left.

As soon as she did, his mother sidled back into the room. 'Now, this girl, she is so khandaani, why couldn't you have married her?'

'Ma, she's married with children,' he said irritatedly.

'Theek hai, but she is the type of woman you should be with. Polished and accomplished.'

In short, a younger version of yourself, thought Vishnu with, he confessed, more than a little discomfort. 'Ma, I have to go out, I'll be back a little late.'

As he drove out, he called up Janaki. He suddenly wanted to talk to her, hear her irreverent take on the situation he found himself in. 'Janaki, Vishnu here. Baby, can you meet me tonight? I need you.' Janaki was more than a little surprised at the call; she thought that Vishnu was deliberately going slow with her.

'Sure sweetheart, where?'

He mentioned a restaurant near her place. 'I'll take some time getting there, I've got to finish up some work,' she said.

'That's all right, I'll get there and call you,' he said.

~

As he walked into the dimly lit Chinese restaurant, Vishnu scanned the room and headed straight for the bar. 'Do you have Blender's?' He took the drink and, nursing it, hunched over the bar, Vishnu wondered why he still felt so vulnerable towards Gayatri.

That's what he said to Janaki, as they sat across the table and nibbled on starters. Janaki raised her eyebrows. 'Are you sure you don't want to get back together with her?'

'Look, this is why I wondered whether I should tell you or not. Janaki, I want you, not her. But we have a history and it's a little difficult to get over that.'

'Is it?' she asked, raising an eyebrow. As he started to say something again, she said, 'Listen, this is okay. As far as I can see, you did not initiate this with her; she came to you. Vishnu, my advice, if you don't want to get involved with her, is to not meet her. I know women; she is going through a rough patch and it suits her to pile on to you.'

'I can't not help her.'

Janaki frowned. 'What kind of help has she asked for? A lawyer's number?'

'No, but maybe she needs someone to talk to.'

Janaki threw in the towel and said, 'Fine then, go over to her place on Saturday and we will take an extended rain check on our meeting, okay?' She stood up.

Vishnu frowned and, as he later realized, was filled with dread when he saw her anger. 'Hey, sit down, will you. Don't behave like a child, please, talk to me!' He grabbed her hand and made her sit down. 'Don't you ever create this kind of scene again, Janaki.'

Janaki sat down, but was plainly sulking. 'Vishnu, I just get upset when even a smart guy like you can't see beyond the tears. That woman just wants to use you to get out of a difficult situation of her own making.'

'We won't talk about it any more, darling. I want to be with you, you know that,' he said gently.

Janaki appeared mollified, but as she sat through dinner and went back home she realized that he still intended to 'help' Gayatri. Why the hell doesn't anyone want to help *me*, she thought to herself. As she recalled Gayatri from a couple of weeks ago, she didn't look at all vulnerable. She looks quite capable of scaling any mountain, Janaki thought. And now she wants my guy. She sighed and thought it served her right for throwing over Saurabh for Vishnu. Welcome to Hindu guilt, she thought.

Nine

The iftar party, or a political version of breaking the Ramadan fast before Eid, at socialist leader Syed Moazzim's house was in full flow. The prime minister and several ministers in the government had made an appearance; Moazzim's stock as host, if not as politician, appeared to be soaring. The pictures from the party would duly appear in the next day's papers.

Janaki and Shakira, both of whom had been invited to the iftar, circulated among the guests. Picking up snippets of gossip, political and otherwise, was the first tool of political reporting despite all attempts by journalists to give it a more serious hue.

Janaki was chatting with some of the officials attached to the offices of the external affairs minister when she spotted Uday Pratap. He stood glowering in a corner, a glass of juice in hand, surrounding by fawning reporters, and his gaze was directed at her. Janaki was startled to say the least. Turning her back to him, for he was making her distinctly uncomfortable, she made her way to where street chaat was being served.

She had barely stuffed a spicy golgappa into her mouth when Uday Pratap appeared beside her. 'So this is where you get your pungent writing skills, huh?' he asked, picking up a bowl.

Janaki choked and the spicy water of the golgappa went cascading down her throat, burning her oesophagus like a bush fire. She coughed for a good five minutes before someone, likely Uday Pratap himself, gave her some orange juice to cool

down her flaming innards. 'Did you have to do that?' she asked
querulously.

He smiled. 'Actually, I did. I hope that discomfort is nothing
compared to mine while watching you consort with these shady
characters.'

'Shady characters? Sir, these are your people, I make my living
out of being a witness to their careers,' she said, her calm restored
after the orange juice.

'I hope you don't think I am like the rest of them.'

'Actually, I don't think of you at all,' she said defiantly. Hell, if
he wanted to flirt, she could cross swords with the best of them, she
thought to herself.

'Really, you don't, huh?' he asked with an amused smile. 'Liar.
I bet you are wondering what it would be like to be with me,' he
whispered, leaning into her.

'You know, I had heard that they served vodka golgappas at
Punjabi by Nature. Are they the caterers here by any chance?' she
asked, moving away and fluttering her eyelashes at him.

Uday Pratap's laughter rang out loud, prompting several people
to turn and stare.

She took little notice of the attention but added for good
measure, 'I seem to remember a very flirty phone call I received a
few days ago, after you'd imbibed a little . . .'

'My dear girl, I can drink from your eyes,' he answered,
unfazed.

'Eesh! That is such a corny line! That's the trouble with men
your vintage, dust off some better lines, please,' she said teasingly.

He laughed again. 'Listen, let's ditch this crowd and have dinner
out.'

Iftar's normally started just before the evening prayers; the food
was served at twilight after that. Political dos like iftars and Diwali
and Holi milans ended early, the object being to see the kind of a
crowd you could rustle up if you were a wannabe host, and
whether you got an invitation if your host had already arrived on
the political scene.

Janaki looked steadily back at Uday Pratap. 'I think we've gone over this terrain, sir, its inappropriate.'

'But you've challenged me to come up with better lines,' he replied, trying to be persuasive.

Before Janaki could respond, Vijay Pratap Singh of *Dainik Samachar* sidled up to Uday Pratap. 'Sir, is it true that the state chief's post in Uttar Pradesh will be given to Kalyan Mishra? Ek bhi Thakur vote nahin milega, sir.'

Uday Pratap just smiled and replied, 'Thakuron ke liye hum hain, bhai,' and, patting Vijay Singh on the back, turned to face Janaki again. Janaki, whose ears had pricked at this news, asked Vijay Singh whether the rumour was very strong.

'Pata nahin, I've heard that this is happening. Baki Thakur sahib will say,' he said, deferentially nodding towards Uday Pratap.

While Indian politics ran on caste lines, it was a loosely held secret that Indian political journalism also ran on similar parochial lines. There was Vijay Singh, who had aligned himself with another Thakur, Uday Pratap, and hung around him in an imitation of a court, while Uday Pratap's main rival Dushyant Trivedi, a Brahmin leader from the same state, held court among mostly Brahmin reporters, in another corner of the lawn.

Knowing a south Indian language got you entry into several ministries where south Indian ministers presided, whereas Malayalam was the language of all seasons, since the gatekeepers and secretarial staff to almost the entire elite of the city were from Kerala. Knowing a smattering of Malayalam was almost as important as knowing some of the libel laws.

Janaki's attention, fixed until that point on Uday Pratap, was now firmly focused on what Vijay Singh had said. Much as she was tempted to take Uday Pratap's offer, her instinct told her that the story would trigger a mini revolt in the state unit of the party, so she needed to get back to office fast.

'Can I take a rain check on dinner?' she asked Uday Pratap.

'What happened?'

'A story was discussed in front of you and you're asking me what happened!' she said even as she started dialling Simran's number to book space for her story. 'I've gotta go, catch you later!'

Janaki called up some of her sources, minor functionaries in the state unit, and confirmed that Vijay Singh's news was indeed correct and that a group of dissidents planned to resign from the party after the announcement in the next couple of days.

Janaki walked back into office and rattled off 350 words on the issue. If the NRP, the party in power in UP, had trouble from within, it had implications for the government. All across the office, there seemed to be hectic activity as the paper's deadline for releasing pages to the printers was nearing. Subeditors and news editors were running around with printouts of pages and checking for last-minute mistakes.

Janaki rechecked her story and released it to the desk. It was only then that she bothered to look at her phone. There were three missed calls from Uday Pratap and a message that read: 'Thrown over for a news story, you cldnt have hurt me more if you tried. Demand restitution for this.'

She smiled and decided not to respond. Frankly, despite the excitement of being chased by this powerful man, she was convinced that it was utterly the wrong thing to do. Her father, a phlegmatic man of few words, always said 'never shit where you eat'. Loosely translated this meant never mix business with pleasure. Although a little harmless flirting on the phone is actually medically recommended if your boyfriend is busy wiping another woman's tears, a wicked inner voice whispered, drowning out her father's virtuous blandishments. It's all Vishnu's fault, it added for good measure.

Ten

Saturday dawned bright and sunny, with fine weather and that nippy feel in the air Delhi got in the autumn, just before the winter hit. Janaki took a long shower and washed her hair and, as she got ready, wished that the butterflies in her stomach would calm down. It wasn't like this was her first time, but with Vishnu she felt all sorts of apprehensions.

Across town Vishnu was having the hardest time getting out of the house. 'Beta, at least spend one Saturday with your mother,' Indira Singh said almost as a plea.

'Ma, please, I need to get somewhere. We'll have dinner together, okay?' He hadn't wanted to have dinner out that night but it seemed his mother wouldn't stop her nagging till he did.

'Okay, beta, if that's the time you can spare for your mother,' she said resignedly.

This was one of the oldest tricks that mothers used to make their children feel guilty. Vishnu protested, 'Ma, please, don't be like that,' and sat down with her. His phone beeped a message. 'Oye, waiting,' it said, and it was from Janaki. He had to pick her up from a common point near Ranbir's house and they would continue in his car. He patted his mother's hand, hugged her and left. It took him a good twenty-five minutes to reach Janaki, who was standing around sipping a latte looking beautiful in a demure salwar kameez.

'Hi,' he said. 'I'm so sorry to be late, baby, my mother . . .' he trailed off and sighed.

Janaki shrugged and got into the car. 'Oh, sorry, did you want some coffee?' she asked.

Vishnu frowned and said no. When a woman does not react to an apology you can take it for granted that she is truly pissed off, someone had once said to him.

'Are you angry with me?' he asked, and almost cursed himself for laying himself open to an angry tirade.

'Nope, you said your mother detained you,' she said formally. Just then her phone rang, and she picked it up and said, 'Sorry, the call dropped suddenly. Did you manage to get a nice guitar?' Then, giggling and laughing, she proceeded to chat with whoever it was for a good fifteen minutes.

When she hung up, they were nearly there, and it was Vishnu's turn to be a little pissed off. 'Had a good chat?' he asked sarcastically.

'Oh yes, we were chatting as I was waiting for you, I could hardly stop once you turned up.'

'Hmmm,' he said, getting the point but still pissed off. 'Who was it?'

'Oh, just Uday Pratap Singh, the NRP MP. He'd called up a couple of weeks ago. His son is learning the guitar and he wanted to pick up a new one,' she said nonchalantly. Inside though, she was seething. She had been planning this day for weeks and this man had had the guts to keep her waiting.

'What are you, an agent for an instruments shop?'

'How dare you use that tone with me? At least I answered a genuine query, and didn't fall for crocodile tears!'

'Oh, so that's what this is all about, is it?' As they entered Ranbir's building and got into the lift, they were still arguing. Vishnu fished out the keys and let them in, still in the middle of the fight. The flat was a typical upwardly mobile residence with wooden flooring, white couches and gilt-edged crown moulding. A little Punjabi for Janaki's tastes, but she really didn't care.

'So what you are saying is that I should forget everything about Gayatri,' he said as he turned to face her.

'What I'm saying is, just shut up and kiss me, you cussed man,' Janaki said and reached up to kiss him. They kissed for the longest time and Vishnu's hands held on to her face before going all over her body.

'Now that's my girl,' he said breathlessly against her.

'Just shut up and don't patronize me,' she replied and got his shirt out of his waistband. He put his hands under her kurta to get at her bra strap, which, as luck would have it, was a front clasp, Janaki giggled and guided his hands and somehow they found themselves in the bedroom.

As clothes flew off, the anger changed to passion. Vishnu looked at Janaki and groaned, 'God, woman, you were made for me!'

'You don't mind my jiggly belly?'

'I love everything about you . . .' he said as he kissed her stomach. 'You are so beautiful!' he whispered as he touched her everywhere.

'You're very beautiful too . . .' Janaki said as her hands skimmed all over his body.

'Er . . . you don't want to go there if you want this to last longer than five minutes,' he said as her hands strayed to where his erection was.

'Now that's a challenge. Rise to the occasion, sir,' she said with a mischievous glint in her eyes and proceeded to not only touch him but tantalize him with her hands and mouth. As her nails raked his inner thighs, Vishnu groaned and dragged her up for a deep kiss.

'Okay, no more.' He flipped her on her back, his hands straying to her sex, where he found she was quite ready for him. He entered her and felt her warmth engulf him; as her legs wrapped around him he promised himself and her that he would do his best to keep this woman, who had brought love and joy back into his life.

'I love you, baby . . .' he whispered to her.

'I love you too.'

He closed his eyes and for a long time all that could be heard in the room were whispered sighs and groans till they both went quiet.

'Okay, that was longer than five minutes, Mr Singh. It means that you can be full of surprises when you apply yourself,' she said, cradled in his arms. She could feel laughter rippling through his chest, under her face and smiled. As they both lazed around, he asked her, 'I hope you meant what you said.'

'About you lasting more than five minutes? Sure.'

He gently slapped her on her bottom and said, 'Enough of your smart mouth, I meant about you loving me.'

She looked up at him and said, 'What do you think?'

'Don't answer a question with a question,' he said, gently squeezing her throat in play.

'Yes,' she said, suddenly serious.

'Then listen to what I have to say. I love you, and don't want to fight about Gayatri again. She meant the world to me, but it is you I love. I can't ignore her though when she has asked for my help.'

As usual, when she came up against a firm opinion, Janaki went silent.

'Okay, I hear you.' She got off the bed and padded to the bathroom.

'Hey, where are you going?'

'To the bathroom. And after that I'm having some lunch,' she said over her shoulder.

As she looked at herself in the bathroom mirror, she knew in her gut that Gayatri would be one of the fault lines in their relationship. 'We'll cross the bridge when we come to it,' she said as she washed up.

When she came out she could hear him talking on the phone to someone, that someone being Gayatri.

'Er, why don't you have dinner with my mother and me at home, Gayatri?'

Janaki raised her eyebrows and put on some clothes. She went into the lobby of the apartment where her bag of sandwiches had been dropped in their race to the bedroom. She rooted around in the bag for her vegetarian sandwich, and coolly served herself some white wine to go with it from Vishnu's bag.

As Vishnu came into the dining room he found Janaki calmly sipping wine and munching on her sandwich.

'Umm, that was Gayatri. She was feeling low so she called.'

Janaki just nodded and offered him some wine. 'Build up your strength partner, we're getting on the carousel again,' she said with a smile. Vishnu frowned at her, it was at moments like these that he felt at a loss. At that point, he felt that she just didn't care; any other girl would have been screaming blue murder.

'So you are okay with her calling me up like that,' he said biting into his sandwich.

Janaki took a deep breath. 'Vishnu, when you've made it clear that my objecting to it is not going to make you stop, is there really any point in my making a fuss? You don't want me to be involved but you want me to be jealous? Is that what you want?'

'You know, you should watch what you say. You can really hurt,' he said to her, but ashamed at the same time because that was exactly what he wanted.

She smiled at him and got up to sit on his lap. As she held his face between her hands, he looked into her brandy eyes and knew he was a goner.

～

Janaki's brandy eyes were all Vishnu could think of as he struggled through dinner with his mother and Gayatri.

'Beta, have some keema, you know you like it.'

He nodded and found Gayatri heaping keema on his plate. 'Thanks,' he said.

As his mother and Gayatri talked about some mutual acquaintances, his mind wandered to Janaki and what she was up to. This afternoon had been amazing, and he couldn't wait to see her again. I owe Ranbir one, he thought, making a mental note to send around a bottle of whisky as a thank-you note.

'Vishnu?' came Gayatri's voice, prompting him out of his reverie. He looked up with a start and saw that he had been steadily shoving food in his mouth and his plate was quite clean. 'I need to wash my hands,' he said and fled the table.

When he got back to the drawing room, he saw that his mother and Gayatri had been sipping coffee. He suddenly wished that it was Janaki here with him now. Instead of retiring to his cold bed, he would be curling up with her, spooned against her back, holding on to that jiggly belly for dear life.

Silly woman, what jiggly belly, he thought with a smile.

'What is so amusing, hamein bhi batao,' said Gayatri.

'Nothing, yaar,' he said hastily. Janaki was his precious secret; he didn't want anyone to know of her just yet.

The object of his thoughts, meanwhile, found that whatever exhaustion she had been battling on the way home had disappeared in a pop. Dave Houghton had responded to her email. He wrote that he had put in a written request for information with the UK land registry office on the source of funding for the two properties Janaki had mentioned. 'These are prime properties, my dear; I went there and checked them out myself,' his email said.

Janaki quickly wrote back that she wanted to know who was on the boards of directors of each of these trusts, where they got funding from and who they funded in turn. She suspected that an arms company was behind these trusts and that the funds for paying kickbacks were being channelled through the trusts.

Within twenty-four hours of being with Vishnu, Janaki had been made aware of two major fault lines in their relationship: his feelings for Gayatri and the story that she was working on. And she knew that the other woman was not as big a problem as her story.

Right now, though, she was sleepy as hell; a warm bath and a bed beckoned her. She refused to think of Vishnu and Gayatri bonding over dinner; instead, she fixed some khichdi for herself, scoffed it down and curled up to sleep.

Despite the day's developments, she soon fell into a deep, dreamless sleep.

Eleven

The next day was Sunday, but Janaki was woken up bright and early by the insistent ringing of her phone. Groggily, she looked at her bedside clock. It was 5.30 a.m., early even by her standards. She picked up the phone and snarled, 'Whoever it is had better have a good reason for buggering up the best sleep I've ever had.'

'Er . . . Janaki? It's Uday Pratap here,' came a hesitant voice at the other end.

'Oh, sorry sir,' she said as she scrambled out of the bedclothes and clutched the phone closer to her ear.

'No, no, I know it's very early for you, but I am going off to Lucknow by the evening flight, and wanted to meet up with you before that. I need to pick up a few books for my sons. Would you be kind enough to help me choose them, at Bahrisons maybe?'

'Me?' Janaki couldn't keep the surprise out of her voice. 'Sir, are you sure? By the way, Khan Market is shut on Sundays,' she said, hoping that this would bring this particular surreal experience to an end. After Friday, she thought she had made things amply clear to him.

'Really? Well, I'm never here on Sundays so I didn't know. We can go to Noida or one of the malls in south Delhi. I'll send my car over at around eleven. We can even grab some brunch. What do you say? Meeting in daylight may make my lines more palatable,' he said with a laugh.

Janaki looked at her phone again and wondered again whether

she was having a dream. She had always maintained a professional distance from politicians and others on her beat, and suddenly she was being asked out for brunch.

'Ummm . . . I guess. Are you sure though?'

'What's not to be sure about? Janaki, I want your opinion on some reading material for my children, that is all.' Janaki nodded but she was sharp enough to know that this was a completely lame excuse; the man was up to something.

'Fine sir, 11 a.m. it is.' After that, she tried to go back to sleep but couldn't; it preyed on her mind that she couldn't figure out this particular deal. She was clear-eyed enough about herself to know that she wasn't exactly god's gift to womanhood, so there was no way that this man was hitting on her. So what was behind all this friendliness?

It was nine thirty by the time Vishnu deigned to call her. Janaki picked up the phone while picking out her outfit—her vanity wouldn't permit her to look anything less than fabulous even for an outing she couldn't figure out. 'Hi,' she said a little breathlessly while picking out a top to go with her linen pants.

'Hey beautiful. Did my baby sleep well?' he asked her teasingly.

'Yes, except that I was woken at the unearthly hour of five thirty and asked to pick out books.'

'By whom?' he demanded to know.

'Uday Pratap. It seems he wants me to help him pick out books for his sons,' she said, knowing as she said it that it would set off a fight between them She couldn't blame him; even she couldn't figure out what this was about.

'What are you, the nanny?'

'Look, even I don't know why he wants to meet up. This is what he said. I want to know what he is up to. And it's not as though we have anything planned for Sunday,' she added for good measure.

Vishnu winced at the accusation, since it was true that Janaki had wanted to catch a film this afternoon and, as usual, his mother had lassoed him into another boring long-winded lunch at their club.

'Listen, whatever it is, I don't like this thing. I want to know what this guy is up to.'

'Me too. There is something at work here.'

'Yeah, like a giant hard-on,' he said crudely.

'Vishnu!' Janaki said, a little shocked at the crudity. 'Aisa nahin hai, just because you think I'm pretty doesn't mean everyone else does. Plus, this guy is a politician; they are made of titanium, so there are wheels within wheels. I need to know.'

'I don't like this, and you are not going to go out with him.'

'Oh yeah? Did I stop you from seeing Gayatri?'

There was silence at the other end. 'Fine then. I think this conversation is not going anywhere. Suit yourself. Bye.' Vishnu hung up on her.

Janaki thought it was fair that, if her concerns were not being taken into account, she was free to follow her own path. She got dressed and, sure enough, a car turned up for her at 11 a.m.

'Hi,' Uday Pratap said to her as she entered the car. 'You are looking very pretty.'

'Thanks,' said Janaki, and saw that he was dressed casually in jeans and a T-shirt.

'You look good too,' she said cheekily.

He grinned at her and shrugged. 'One tries.'

As they drove towards the city, they talked about the state of the traffic in Delhi and moved on to general chit-chat. They entered a mall in south Delhi and headed for the bookshop there. As they browsed through the children's section, they picked out a few books that even Janaki had heard were good. She also forced him to pick out Tolkein and C.S. Lewis for his elder son. 'He'll love it, I'm telling you.'

He smiled at her. 'You know I had a very dog-eared copy of Narnia at home. I don't know where it is.'

'Your wife could look for it.'

'I don't think she'd know where it is.'

Janaki frowned a little at that. After they paid for the books, they escaped from the Sunday crush in the mall. They decided that they would grab lunch at a central Delhi hotel.

They settled themselves at their table and went over their purchases. Janaki decided to grab the bull by the horns. 'You know you could have done this by yourself. Why did you need me?'

'Janaki, I knew I didn't fool you. I'll be honest, I wanted to see you, especially after Friday evening. We have been speaking on the phone and we've met a couple of times. I find that I am drawn to you. I'll be honest, I'm not someone who is very sentimental but we have a connection.'

Janaki was a little flustered by the admission. She had been expecting some grilling on the progress of the story, or even a very plainly stated proposition, but not this. 'Umm . . . sir, I don't know what to say. You are married.'

'I know that, Janaki,' he said and looked deep into her eyes.

Heaven help me, why does this have to happen to me now? Janaki wailed to herself. She realized with a jerk that she felt a flicker of interest when he looked at her with those penetrating eyes. What is wrong with me, she said to herself.

As if sent just to snap her out of her almost hypnotic trance, she suddenly spotted Vishnu and Gayatri walk into the restaurant and sit down directly across from them. Janaki's eyes widened, but she was quick to hide her chagrin, since Vishnu was on Purushottamam's staff and she didn't want Uday Pratap to know about it.

So she decided to distract him. 'Please don't tell me you have an unhappy marriage, it would be the confirmation of all sorts of clichés.'

Uday Pratap smiled. 'No, I have a more or less happy marriage. Nobody forced me into it and we've had a good run till now. What I want to tell you is that I have been drawn to you, since the day we met.'

'Sir,' she started.

'Oh for god's sake, Janaki, please call me by my name!'

'Okay, Uday, I'm involved with someone and you're married. While I do admit that at another time I would have fallen hook, line and sinker, but I don't see that happening right now. And, frankly, I don't believe you. I have a very healthy and realistic idea of who I am.'

Uday Pratap smiled at that, and said, 'I don't know what kind of man you are involved with, but, for me, I can say that I find you extremely appealing and attractive, and very, very sexy.'

She frowned at him, and said, 'Uday, you are very attractive yourself, you know that; don't play around like this. I am not from your world; I don't know your rules and won't play by them. Don't be unkind,' she said wearily.

Uday Pratap's face fell. He held her hand across the table and said, 'Janaki, I didn't mean to upset you like this, sweetheart. I just . . . I just wanted to tell you how I felt. I hope you don't think I'm some sort of shyster or playboy; I don't do this as a norm. It's just that I seem to be living my life in pieces, one part in Lucknow, another as a politician here, then there is my life with my family, and I don't know at what point to bring this all together. When I met you, it was like something clicked.'

All Janaki was aware of was Vishnu and Gayatri talking intensely across the table.

Delhi really is a village, she thought to herself. They couldn't find another restaurant or what, for the second time in a row!

She brought back her attention to Uday Pratap, gently disengaging her hand from his. 'Uday, please don't misunderstand me. I find it difficult to believe that someone worldly like you would find me appealing. I didn't mean to impugn your reputation, although you are a married man,' she said with a smile. 'This could just be a mid-life crisis,' she said teasingly.

He smiled a little, but sighed and said, 'Janaki, think about it, we could be good together. I seriously feel very happy and relaxed with you.'

Janaki just shook her head. 'I think I need to leave now.'

'Certainly. I'll drop you home.'

They got up. Janaki could feel a hard stare on her back all the way out; she knew Vishnu had seen them together, but she too was pissed off with him. At least I told him who I was going out with. Hmph, going out with his mother indeed! she thought to herself. Just to make him feel like a heel, she turned around, looked directly at him and glared. He looked back at her, their gaze held, and it was as though it was just the two of them, like the previous afternoon.

Janaki broke the gaze and followed Uday Pratap out and into the waiting vehicle. All the way back to her house, her mind was in turmoil. She wrestled with the fact that she loved one man and was also attracted to another. The very fact that Uday Pratap came from a world that was unfamiliar to her in its intimacy—she never met politicos outside work—was part of the appeal; she was honest enough to admit it to herself,

She sneaked a look at Uday Pratap, who was also looking at her intensely. Suddenly he said to his driver, 'Mahinder, you get off here. I will drive madam home.'

Janaki was a little startled. They stopped on the side of a road to make the switch. Uday Pratap gave his driver some money to take an autorickshaw and they both settled in the front seat of the car.

He started the car and, just like Vishnu, held her hand, even while changing gears. Janaki felt strangely detached, as if she were having an out-of-body experience—it was just so surreal. He turned and smiled at her and kissed her hand. As he deftly manoeuvred the car through the streets, Janaki just looked at him, a little bemused. Near her place, he stopped in a bylane, and gathered her close to him. 'I can't let you go without doing this,' he whispered, and, in broad daylight, kissed her deeply.

Janaki closed her eyes, letting the feelings rush through her. It was gentle and savage at the same time, there was tongue but there were teeth as well. And she was surprised that, this man, who had all the reason in the world to fear discovery was kissing her on a street side with the sun shining in all its glory.

When they broke off, he looked at her, his breathing a little laboured. 'Now say you don't want this to go any further.'

'I don't want this to go any further,' she parroted.

He hugged her to him, and whispered in her ear, 'Why, sweetheart? We would be so good together!'

'Uday, don't do this. I'm involved with someone I love; you and I are impossible, and I don't do impossible.'

'What do you mean you don't do impossible?' he asked her, tucking her hair behind her ear.

'Just that I'm twenty-eight, and I don't need to be involved with a forty-one-year-old married man who will never leave his wife,' she said stonily.

'My god, you are cynical; you don't feel anything, no magic!'

'Uday, you can take it any way you like it: I am not convinced of your feelings for me and I am in love with someone else. The reason I'm calmly necking in this car is because I'm taken aback by the fact that I can be with two guys at the same time.'

He seemed to lose his temper at that. 'This man you keep harping about, you must not want him very much to be with me like this.'

'You can think whatever you want, Uday; you and I are not happening.'

He started the car and drove the rest of the way in stony silence. She got off quietly and said, 'I hope your kids enjoy the books. Bye,' and walked into the gate.

The security guard at the gate was waiting for her. 'Madam someone has come to see you; he's waiting outside your flat. I have sent Jaiveer to stand guard there with him.'

Oh? Janaki thought, it can't be Saurabh, these people know him well. 'Theek hai,' she said to the guard.

There, outside her door, stood Vishnu, and he didn't look pleased. Fortunately he didn't say a word while she dismissed the second security guard, fished around in her bag for her keys, and opened the door to let him in. She was still in a daze and Vishnu's sudden appearance had further confused her.

'Would you like to sit?' she said very softly, gesturing to a chair.

'What I'd like to do is to give you a sound thrashing, woman. How dare you hold hands with another guy after being with me,' he said to her softly, menacing.

Janaki looked straight at Vishnu. 'The same way that you could go out with another woman, after having told me that you would be with your mother.'

'Janaki, that was a last-minute thing. Gayatri turned up and Ma dropped out,' he said running his hands through his hair.

'Whatever it was, I told you I was going out with Uday Pratap Singh. You didn't tell me that you were on such familiar terms with your ex-girlfriend,' she said, now slowly burning up with anger again.

'I don't owe you an explanation for that, I have already explained whatever I had to. Just tell me why the hell that son of a bitch was getting familiar with you?' he said and got up, suddenly towering over her.

'So you don't owe me an explanation, do you? Fine then, think whatever you want, Vishnu, I don't owe you anything either,' she added angrily.

'Like hell you don't,' he said, and, putting his hands on both sides of her face, he drew her in for an angry kiss, all teeth and mashed lips, grinding against her.

Janaki tried to fight him off, hitting him with her fists, but he just grabbed her hands and held them behind her with one hand, and continued to kiss her. His lips moved over her neck nipping little bite marks, which would leave hickeys for sure. And suddenly, the air between them, angry and pulsing, changed to passion as Janaki began to respond. 'Where is your bedroom?' he asked her.

'Why? Can't we do it here?' she replied—she had left the room in a bit of a mess in the morning.

'Have some pity on my back, yaar, I can't take the cold floor. I'm old now,' he said with a laugh.

They kissed and backed their way to her bedroom, where they collapsed on the bed with a whoosh, her clothes—strewn on her bed in her hurry to leave in the morning—getting crushed under their weight.

'Baby, now tell me why you were holding hands with that guy,' he said, looking deep into her eyes.

'Why were you out with that woman?' she asked back.

'You won't tell me?' he asked again.

'No,' she said. 'Either we both discuss this or we both are free to do anything we want.'

'You want to see other people?' he asked as he shoved his hands under her T-shirt to unclasp her bra.

'Only if you are going to.'

'You are not going to see anyone else, madam,' he said with a growl.

'You'd better shape up then.'

All this time clothes were being flung about the room. Vishnu couldn't understand why she couldn't just say she wouldn't see that joker again. 'Why can't you just say you won't see him again?' he asked as he gently bit her along her neck.

'Why can't you?' she said arching her back. He entered her swiftly. Janaki pulled backed a bit at the surprise. 'Oh,' she said, 'like that, is it?'

'Just shut up, if you are not going to say what I want.'

'Fine,' she said moving against him. The battle of wills played out for some time till pleasure claimed the two of them.

As she lay in bed next to Vishnu, listening to his heartbeat now slowing down to normal, Janaki wondered just where this would lead them, and just how she could explain anything to Vishnu, when she herself was clueless as hell.

He propped himself up on his elbow and asked her, 'Why won't you refuse to see him again?'

Janaki looked into his eyes and said, 'Because he's part of my beat, I can't ignore him.'

'Last I heard journalism did not involve going on shopping trips with sources.'

'That is correct. Last I heard, when a man says he can't take the woman he loves to the movies because he has to have lunch with his mother, she doesn't expect to see him romancing his ex.'

'I already explained to you about that.'

'So have I. In fact, you knew I was seeing Uday; your outing was a complete ambush.'

'It's Uday now, is it?' he said, the jibe clear in his voice.

'Vishnu, either I am important enough to you for you to stop seeing that woman, or you stop questioning me about what I do. If you are going to suit yourself, and it is that kind of relationship you are offering me, then you have to swallow that pill as well.'

Vishnu was very quiet. He couldn't understand why Janaki was refusing to listen to him. 'These politicians are not like us, Janaki, nothing touches them really.'

'Don't be patronizing, Vishnu, I am aware of their true nature. And don't think that just because someone smiles at me I melt. Married women with children who get back in touch with their exes are never that innocent either,' she retorted.

'What do you want me to do? I cared for her, Janaki, very much, I can't turn my back on her now!' he said with a slightly raised voice. 'She is a sweet woman in a tough situation. She hasn't given me leave to confide in anyone about her troubles.'

'Fine then, don't tell me what to do either.'

Vishnu sighed, and didn't say anything. He got up and started to put on his clothes. Then he turned around and said, 'Janaki, it hurt me to see you with another man. I love you, sweetheart.'

'Vishnu, I stand by what I said. This is not a one-way street,' she replied. Even as she said it, she wondered whether it would not be an altogether bad thing to give in, but Gayatri's patrician features flashed before her eyes. She was damned if she would stand by and allow another man to walk over her! 'You know what you have to do, and so do I.'

Vishnu sighed again and, tucking his shirt into his waistband, said, 'You are really very stubborn.'

'I never said I was a pushover.'

At this Vishnu simply walked out of the door.

Janaki lay back in bed, and wondered whether she had done the right thing in holding on to her view. As always, she needed to bounce this off Kajal. Janaki and Kajal were very clear on certain things, they told each other everything, so while Vishnu was the man she loved, he would never be told about the kiss with Uday, but Kajal would.

'Hi Kaj,' said Janaki as Kajal picked up the phone. 'Where are you, dudette?'

'At Ambience, there is a humongous sale on, Janaki, you sooooo have to check it out,' she said as shrieks and cries were heard in the background.

'Is that a sale or a massacre?' Janaki said with a laugh.

'Kuch bhi samajh le, it's war over a pair of tights here. Kya hua, why'd you call?'

'I need to talk. Can we meet up for some coffee later?'

'Code red or orange,' asked Kajal, orange being the really serious one.

'Is it ever anything less than orange with me,' Janaki said, misery dripping from her voice.

'Hmmm, okay, I am driving towards the city in the evening. Let's meet at Fez for a drink?' Fez, a Middle Eastern joint in the diplomatic area of Chanakyapuri, was a favourite hang-out for both of them.

'You're on,' Janaki said.

~

It was seven when Janaki walked into Fez, and Kajal was already there, in deep consultation with their waiter.

'Hi,' Janaki said a little breathlessly as she settled into her seat. 'I've ordered a mojito pitcher, and some mezze, is that okay?' Kajal asked her.

'Sure.'

'Haan, ab bol,' said Kajal turning her attention to her best friend.

'Oh Kaj, I'm in a bit of a mess actually,' said Janaki and the whole sorry tale just poured out of her.

'Hmm . . . My, my, you certainly seem to be on a roll, Janaki,' Kajal said with a wink and a salute with her cocktail.

'Oye, be serious yaar, help me out.'

'Dekh, you seem to be attracted to both guys, am I right?'

'Yes.'

'But you love Vishnu, he is like, the One, right?'

'Yes to that as well.'

'It's simple really. The politico is a bad idea, however seductive he might appear. Vishnu is single, loves you, totally your type and you see a future with him.'

Janaki nodded. 'But what about this business with the ex?'

'Yeah, that could be a problem, because, of all women, you cannot carry off the bechara look, and you know that tears always win,' said Kajal sympathetically. 'You will just say you will cope, and the guy will lay down himself when this chick sheds a couple of tears.'

'What should I do?' asked Janaki, now genuinely upset—she could just see Vishnu walking into a Coca-Cola sunset with Gayatri gently wiping her tears on a snowy handkerchief. 'I can learn to cry.'

'Nah, tujhse nahin hoga,' said Kajal unsympathetically. 'You'd better stick to your hammer approach, less grief for you. If he really is as great as you say, he'll see through her soon enough. In either case, Janaki, there is no point in reacting like someone else; if you are upset, then that's the way it is. He will have to deal with it.'

Janaki nodded, Gayatri did disturb her.

Well, what about that clinch in the car with Uday, doesn't Vishnu deserve to know about that? said a voice in her head. Tamping it down viciously, Janaki sipped her cocktail.

'Kajal, why do you think this is so, yaar, shouldn't being with one prevent me from being with the other? I feel its really slutty of me, yaar,' she said with a sigh.

Kajal smiled and said, 'Thoda bahut toh hai!' Janaki threw a napkin at her in mock anger.

'I really don't know what you are up to, man, but I want a ringside view,' said Kajal with a snort of laughter.

Janaki wailed, 'I wanted to meet you to get a bit of clarity, and you are not helping!'

'Oh, is that why I'm here? I thought I was here for the entertainment,' she chortled.

Janaki pulled a face at her and took a long pull at her cocktail.

Her mind was in turmoil; she had never in her life imagined being in this situation. She loved Vishnu and could see a life with him; with Uday there was just this stomach-clenching excitement.

'I'll think about it later,' she said to herself.

~

Kishoreda was in a very good mood, and especially pleasantly disposed towards Janaki. 'This friend of your father's, he will be able to get you that information, right?' he asked her for the umpteenth time. Janaki nodded and pushed forward her travel requisition for London. Dave Houghton said that he had already put in a request at the UK land registry office, but Janaki needed to physically verify the addresses in Apex's papers.

'Okay, okay, fine. Here, just ask accounts to make sure you have enough foreign exchange for the trip.'

Simran was a little more forthcoming. 'Ask Naveen if he can get you an upgrade to first class after your tickets are booked.' Naveen Uniyal was their civil aviation correspondent and, as such, was called on for any favour to do with air travel.

Janaki nodded miserably, all too aware that the moment the story broke, she would have to answer some really tough questions from Vishnu. He may not even want to talk to me, she thought to herself. As she went to and fro getting her travel documents and foreign exchange sanctions, Janaki kept hoping that she would be taken off the story. All she got, however, was a regulation digital camera from the photography department and a set of instructions on how to use it.

Packing it in her bag, Janaki asked the travel desk for tickets to London for the following weekend. She had some friends studying in the city and she wanted the distraction of a weekend of fun before she got down to business.

As she got back to her workstation, she checked her phone. There were two missed calls from Vishnu. It had been two weeks since that afternoon at her house, and Vishnu and she had more or less made up—a kind of 'don't ask don't tell' policy. They had met up every evening but studiously avoided bringing up either Gayatri or Uday Pratap. Curiously, it had worked for them, and, despite Vishnu's continuous reservations over what he termed Janaki's 'crass sense of humour', they got along just fine. They did the conventional thing—went out for movies, played pool, went to a couple of nightclubs and discovered that they had fun when a third person was not mentioned.

Janaki often wished that Vishnu had a different boss, or at least that it was Deepak and not her breaking the story.

As she called Vishnu back, Janaki wondered whether full disclosure wouldn't be such a bad thing after all, what with her upcoming trip and the fact that the story would break within a week of her return.

Vishnu's question when he answered stopped her in her tracks completely.

'Hi,' he said, a little breathlessly.

'Hi, what's up?'

'Umm . . . I was wondering, would you be free tomorrow evening after seven?'

'I'll try and finish early. What do you have in mind?'

'Could you come home and meet my mother?' he asked, completely shocking Janaki. Vishnu had waxed eloquent on the subject of his mother, the formidable Indira Singh. Widowed when Vishnu had just finished high school, she had held on to their ancestral land and wealth in the face of great opposition from Vishnu's uncles.

Beautiful in the conventional sense, Indira had a core of steel and an innate feminine style of getting her way in everything, something that alternately fascinated and repelled her son in equal measure. Janaki always thought that it was a miracle that Vishnu decided to pursue her considering the fact that both his mother and his ex-girlfriend appeared to be made from the same mould.

'Er, sure. But do you think that is a good idea? I mean, we've only been dating three months.' Janaki felt very protective of their relationship, and didn't want the added strain of meeting Indira Singh and shafting Vishnu's boss to happen so close together.

'Why? Are you afraid?' he asked teasingly, but not without a fair bit of sympathy. He had thought long and hard about the matter, and he acknowledged that he had been a little unfair to Janaki over his proximity to Gayatri. By introducing her to his mother, Vishnu hoped she would understand the depth of his feelings for her.

'Would you think less of me if I said no?' asked Janaki with a sigh. 'Seriously, do we need to do this?'

'Janaki, I love you, sweetheart, and I feel we are ready to take this to the next level. The temptation to hide this is great, I know, but we should be a little bold now. Unless you want to move on,' he said suddenly, visions of Janaki with Uday Pratap flashing before his eyes.

'Uff . . . just shut up and tell me where and when,' she said irritably, shutting off that train of thought.

'Just come by seven thirty. I'll text you the exact address.'

'Okay then,' she replied and hung up. Her mind was racing; she was already feeling terribly guilty, and her self-castigation went into overdrive. She couldn't say enough mean things about herself and what she was about to do to Vishnu's career. At the same time, she needed some real advice on how to deal with a potential mother-in-law, even if one knew that the wedding might never take place. Monika flitted by in front of her, and Janaki grabbed her like a drowning man clutching a raft.

'Mon, please, I need your help, desperately.'

'Woh sab to theek hai, but tell me, what will you get for me from London?' asked Monika, ever the mercenary. 'I'll kill you if you say Quality Street candy.'

'I'll get you killer boots, yaar, tu jo maange, but I need help!'

'What happened?' asked Monika, now serious.

'Vishnu wants me to meet his mother.'

'Really? He is so serious about this?'

'Yes, and I'm terrified, yaar. She is supposed to be one of those Thakurain type women, you know. Khandaani, parampara and the likes.'

'Look, as long as Vishnu and you are okay, she could be Lalita Pawar and it would hardly matter. Wear a nice salwar kameez or sari and be polite. That's all there is to it. Vishnu is going to be there, so why is there a problem?'

'What am I going to say?' wailed Janaki.

'She'll ask you questions and you just have to answer them. Don't make the mistake of being very subdued; be yourself, but be polite.'

Janaki nodded. It sounded like good advice—plain and simple. Her mind still boggled at the developments though. Saurabh's mother had known Janaki from college and Saurabh had a fairly desultory relationship with his family, so she had never found herself in this position. Honestly, she was intimidated by the prospect of meeting Indira Singh.

~

Janaki spent the rest of the day preparing for the trip. She figured out her travel plans, booked a hotel and called up Dave Houghton. She discussed her travel plans with him and asked him for a meeting the next day. She needed to go over all the details with him.

'Yes dear, Monday would be good. We can pick up the information from the UK land registry office and then go around checking it out. I must say this is very exciting,' he said with a laugh.

Janaki smiled and replied, 'I'm glad you think so. It terrifies me!'

'Don't worry, dear. We'll figure it all out,' he said and rang off.

Janaki got back to her research into Purushottamam's brother Shanmugham and the details of the aircraft deal. The largest ever order to be placed by the Indian Air Force had generated a lot of interest in arms and aircraft manufacturing companies. After the Bofors scandal, arms purchases were a very tricky affair, but unfortunately still in the hands of middlemen and dealers.

Shanmugham ran an export company, which was getting cash

inflows from some other companies for orders that appeared strange. Even stranger were the property details. There were two office properties listed for the company in London, which also housed the two trusts Janaki knew about. With a business that appeared to be tanking, holding on to two buildings in London's tony Hyde Park was suspicious to say the least.

The story was shaping up fine, and worrying the hell out of Janaki. This may yet determine whether I get to marry the man I love, she thought, and a Kafkaesque feeling washed over her.

She saved her notes, made copies on her pen drive and packed up her computer. She also emailed copies of her notes to two different email accounts just to be on the safe side. As she drove home from the office, she went over all the information she had. Once the UK land registry office names who funds these buildings, the shit will hit the ceiling for sure, she thought to herself.

~

As she let herself into her house, her phone rang. It was Uday Pratap. They hadn't spoken since that Sunday, as Janaki referred to it, and she was a little apprehensive about how to react to him now.

'Hi,' she said, her voice breathy with apprehension.

'Hi. How are you doing, Janaki?' he asked in his deep baritone.

'I'm good. I thought I wouldn't hear from you again,' she said, taking the plunge and looking directly at the elephant in the room.

'I wanted to keep away, but as you can see, I am calling you up. I notice that you didn't call me up even once,' he said, sounding peeved.

'Uday, did you expect it? If you really think about it, it's just your ego which is hurt. You know, and I know, that this is impossible.'

'Actually, I don't know that. And don't patronize me, Janaki, by saying that it's only my ego that's hurt.'

By this time Janaki was actually losing her patience. 'Uday, please. I live in the real world even if you don't, so please, you can't pull this off. It was one kiss; it happened; forget it.'

'Janaki, I'm not so hard up for female company that I'll run after you. If that's the attitude you want to take, then fine, but don't presume to know me or the way I feel.'

'Okay, so how do you feel, Uday? That I'm the answer to all your prayers and that we'll be the next Raj Kapoor and Nargis?'

'Stop with your sarcasm right there, young lady! All I meant was that we have something special, I feel happy around you and we could explore this further.'

'Uday, please! I'm not trying to cheapen what we did, but I love someone else. I am attracted to you, but I will not jeopardize what I have for a fling with you,' she retorted, now moved to anger.

'Janaki, I hope you realize what you are throwing away.'

'I can't believe you don't realize what you are asking of me! I will not be your mistress, Uday,' she said coldly.

There was a heavy sigh at the other end of the line. 'You are right. I don't know what I was thinking. I want you in my bed, Janaki; I don't seem to get why you don't want me.'

'I do want you, Uday, but it's impossible. It can't happen; it's not going to go anywhere.'

'You don't feel even the least bit curious about how we would be in bed?' he asked her, changing tack.

Janaki giggled, the sudden change of mood taking her by surprise. 'Actually, I do, but don't want to pay such a high price for my curiosity.'

'Hey, come off it! You're making me sound like some daaku-type character in a Hindi movie, ready to carry off the village belle and do the dirty with her.'

At this Janaki laughed outright. 'I have been doing that, haven't I?' she said and laughed again. 'I'm sorry, but it's been nagging at me: how I could be attracted to you and still be in love with someone else?'

'Janaki, don't worry yourself about it; it happens. It's more common than you know, and, anyway, it was worth a shot,' he said with a laugh. 'See you around, kid,' he said, signing off.

'Bye,' replied Janaki and hung up the phone.

~

Janaki was still pondering over her conversation with Uday Pratap as she fixed her dinner. She supposed he was right; it happened to everyone, this feeling of being attracted to more than one person. If that's true then everyone keeps mighty quiet about it, she thought.

She was also rather proud that she didn't tell him about her upcoming trip, but she supposed that Kishoreda might have. As the investigation was progressing, Janaki couldn't help feeling that she was being made a patsy in this high-stakes game. But, since she had nothing concrete to go on, she kept her counsel.

As had become usual practice for them, Vishnu called her just after dinner for their postprandial chat. 'Hi baby. Wassup?'

'Vishnu, sweetheart, I'm quaking in my shoes thinking about tomorrow. What if your mother absolutely hates me?'

'Sweetheart, that will make you even more desirable a wife for me, in my eyes,' he chortled.

'Vishnu, be serious!'

'I am being serious, Janaki. I love you, and I'm serious about you. That's all she needs to know. My mother's opinion is her own, and will have no bearing on our plans.'

'Hmm, okay I guess,' she said, still not looking forward to it at all. The rest of the conversation was about how their days had been; Janaki carefully edited out any references to her story, only telling Vishnu that she had an assignment that would require her to travel to London next week.

'Baby, you must meet up with my friend Ashish Mehta there. I'll mail him tonight. He'll take you around; he works in a private equity firm in the City area. He's a great guy and will make sure you're not bored.'

'No, no, I have a few friends I want to meet up with. So it's all right,' Janaki said hurriedly. She was already feeling miserable about the story and its possible impact on Vishnu's career. She didn't want to pile on to his friend on top of it.

'Oh, okay. Make sure you watch a stage show, Janaki. They are expensive but worth it.'

'Anything else my lord wishes me to do?' she asked mockingly.

'Oh Janaki, I wish I was going with you! We would have had fun!'

'We'll go there together later,' she said, hoping that they would still be together after the story broke.

Twelve

Indira Singh raised an eyebrow at Janaki, coldly acknowledging her. Janaki's worst fears seemed to be coming true. Good god, she hates me, she thought to herself.

'So, beta, what did you say your father did?'

They were seated in the formal living room. And while the walls did not exactly have stuffed animals on them, the furniture was extremely formal and gilt-edged, surprising Janaki, as it seemed very unlike Vishnu's taste. Despite it all, there were some nice paintings on the wall, and Janaki spent some time looking at them.

'He taught literature in the University.'

'And your mother now lives in Bangalore, does she?' probed Indira.

'Yes, Aunty.'

'In her own house or rented accommodation?'

Janaki felt like she was in a Nazi interrogation room. 'Own house, Aunty,' she responded calmly.

Indira Singh unbent and gave a small smile. 'You know, beta, Vishnu's father left us very early in life. I have tried my best to give him the best. His happiness is the most important thing in my life.'

'Yes, Aunty, Vishnu told me about his father,' Janaki said, not knowing what else to say. She was, frankly, a little irritated with Vishnu as well, who had introduced the two of them and retired to his study in order to 'finish up some work'.

Indira Singh's line of questioning also was strange. She seems to want to gauge just how well off I am, thought Janaki. She ought to have been incensed by this intrusion, but the feeling of being in a *saas–bahu* soap was so intense that she just blindly answered what she could.

After the few desultory questions about her parents, Indira Singh dropped a bomb. 'Beta, journalism is all fine when you are single, but Vishnu has a transferable job, and, as his wife, you will have to move when he does. How do you see a career as compatible with that? If you were in the same service it would have been fine, but . . .' She trailed off.

'Aunty, that's all quite far away I guess. We haven't really thought so far ahead,' she said, choking over the words in anger. How dare Vishnu leave me alone to face this, she thought to herself.

Indira Singh was not impressed with this sidestepping of her question. 'You will have to think about all this, especially when children come along. This really won't do.'

Janaki barely managed to silence her gasp of dismay at that. Good god, this woman is incorrigible, before long she'll tell me when I can take a toilet break, thought Janaki to herself.

Just as they were about to step into the dining room, where a formally set dinner awaited them, Gayatri walked in. Surprisingly, Janaki's first reaction was not of dismay or jealousy but a kind of detached wonder at the fact that all the things that could go wrong were doing so.

'Hello Aunty, we missed you at the flower show today. Mrs Mehta's dahlias were out of this world,' Gayatri said as she air-kissed Indira Sinha in greeting. Then, turning a remarkably supercilious look on Janaki, she introduced herself. 'Hello, I'm Gayatri Dhar, an old friend of Vishnu's. You are . . . ?'

At that point Vishnu walked in. The look of dismay on his face at seeing Gayatri would have been comical if Janaki had not been seething with anger.

'This is Janaki Rao, a friend of mine,' he said, intervening.

Janaki hardly wanted Vishnu to declare his love from the

rooftops, but to be dismissed as just 'a friend' was also something she couldn't take. She gave him a cold look, thinking to herself that she probably wouldn't have to wait for her story to break. Their relationship would be sunk by these two formidable ladies.

As they settled around the dining table, Indira Singh and Gayatri kept up a steady chatter of small talk about people and events that Janaki had no knowledge of, completely shutting her out. Vishnu shrugged at her helplessly and silently messaged an apology across the table.

Then he intervened in a last-ditch attempt, 'Ma, Janaki's mother is quite an accomplished classical dancer.'

'Really? She has performed on stage, has she?' Indira Singh said, as though that made Mythili Rao just a shade better than an escort.

'She had her *arangetram*, and did a couple of stage shows, but gave up when I came along,' Janaki said bristling at Indira Singh's tone.

Vishnu sensed that this wasn't going the way he wanted it to. Silence prevailed for some more time before his mother and Gayatri again started talking between themselves. Vishnu let it slide, now quite eager to get the evening over with.

As the interminable evening wound to a close, Janaki said her goodbyes to both the ladies. She and Vishnu walked out to the portico of his house in silence, each preoccupied with what had happened this evening.

'Erm . . . Janaki, perhaps this was not such a good idea after all. I really didn't expect Gayatri to turn up,' said Vishnu, a little worried that the two women had put him in the doghouse with Janaki.

Janaki didn't say a word. She was furious and didn't trust herself to be polite. 'Hmm . . .' was all she responded with. 'I'll see myself out, Vishnu,' she said fishing out her car keys and walking briskly off.

'Janaki, wait! I'll walk you to the car at least . . .' he said, his voice trailing off as she walked away fast and got into her car.

As he watched her drive off, a slow burning anger grew in him.

Ma had better have an explanation for this, he said to himself. Vishnu normally avoided confrontations with his mother on any issue, since he knew, and was repeatedly told, of the huge sacrifices she had made for him, but today he just needed to get this off his chest.

As he walked in, the two women were huddled together on the sofa and broke apart as though caught planning a conspiracy. 'Gayatri, I need to speak to my mother alone,' he said in a cold voice.

Gayatri's eyes darted to Indira Singh who promptly said, 'Nonsense, beta, you can say what you want in front of Gayatri.'

'You will not tell me where and in front of whom to speak, Ma. The display of ill-breeding that you two ladies put up today has quite removed any rights you have to lecture me on manners and appropriate behaviour,' he said.

'That girl is not right for you, Vishnu, and our plan today was to show you that. She comes from a different background and will never fit in with our lifestyle.'

'What lifestyle is that, Ma? As far as I know, Janaki comes from the same background: she is educated and independent, things I prize in a woman.'

'Beta, you know what I mean. You've got proposals from good families, consider any of those girls. Gayatri here is an example of the kind of woman you should be with.'

Vishnu saw red. 'Really? If you must know, Ma, Gayatri was my girlfriend ten years ago. She dumped me then, considering me not good enough to marry and now wants me to rescue her from her crappy marriage!'

A gasp from Gayatri made him realize what he had said in anger. 'Yes, madam, you've heard right. Just because I respect what we had doesn't mean I'm an emotional patsy,' he said to her. 'And as for you,' he pointed to his mother, 'you have no idea who I am and what I want. So please don't extend this kind of "help" in the future!'

Vishnu thought this was as good an exit line as any—like all men, he was helpless when confronted by tears, and his mother looked like she was going for the brahmastra. He turned on his heel and walked out.

~

Vishnu got into his car and dialled Janaki's number. He hoped that, unlike other women, she would take his call and not waste his time by rejecting it every time he called.

'Hi.'

'Hi Vishnu,' she said. Vishnu breathed a sigh of relief at her matter-of-fact tone.

'You're really upset with me, aren't you?'

He heard her sigh deeply at the other end. 'Vishnu, you shouldn't have abandoned me to her and then emerged from your room just before dinner. You should have smoothed the process. In any case, I think she was predisposed to not like me. Hardly anyone's fault, but yes, this pain could have been postponed.'

'Look, I've told her off for treating you this way.'

'There's no need to fight with your mother, Vishnu.'

The matter-of-fact tone that had reassured him now made him angry. She seemed unaffected by the whole thing.

'Er, about Gayatri . . .' he began, but Janaki cut him off mid-sentence. 'Leave it, Vishnu, I don't want to talk about this any more.'

'You will bloody well talk about this, woman,' he said, now suddenly angry. After all, all three women could not be angry with him at the same time. 'I've told her off; she won't be a problem any more.'

'Good to know,' she replied sarcastically.

'Can you now tell me on oath that you haven't spoken to Uday Pratap Singh after that day?'

'I spoke to him just this morning, Vishnu, but I don't think the cases are quite comparable. He's not my ex-boyfriend, someone with whom I have a history, and, besides, I have made it very clear that I'm a journalist, not a potential date.'

'So he had that in mind,' Vishnu said triumphantly.

'Whatever he may have had in his mind, it is destined to stay there, and now, I really must hang up. I think there is only so much heaviness a person can take in a day.'

Vishnu looked at the phone and didn't know whether it had gone well or badly. He shrugged and shook his head, deciding that getting piss drunk was the only way out. He headed out to his club, quite at odds with the female sex.

Janaki, meanwhile, was at war with herself. She'd had the perfect opportunity to tell Vishnu about the story that would consume his boss like a tidal wave, but didn't. This is it, I don't think we are going to last, she thought to herself. The slights Indira Singh had dealt out were going to be nothing compared to her transgressions, all in the name of professional duty, ethics and commitments. Sometimes, life just sucks, she thought to herself.

Thirteen

London in November was cold and blustery but fortunately not yet wet and snowy. As Janaki drew her coat close, she consoled herself that at least the weather appeared to be on her side.

'At least it hasn't rained yet,' said Dave Houghton, echoing her thoughts. They were walking towards Hyde Park, having received the information from the UK land registry office, called Companies House, by post.

Janaki's worst fears had been confirmed. Shanmugham's company had listed those very addresses as office space in London. Hillgate and Rothman's Trust also had offices in the same building. As it turned out, according to the registry office records, these trusts had paid for the building. The address information put the headquarters in Lichtenstein, a known tax haven and a conduit for a lot of black money out of India.

This made the story more authentic. Dave and Janaki took up positions near the building and surreptitiously tried to take pictures. London policing depended hugely on hidden CCTV cameras in public places, and any suspicious movements were tracked. An Asian-looking woman taking pictures of buildings in one of London's poshest neighbourhoods would set off alarm bells for sure.

It would be bye-bye Janaki, before I could say al-Qaeda, she thought to herself. 'Uncle, I think you should take the pictures and we should stand apart,' she said.

Dave smiled at her. 'I can see that the journey from Delhi to London has changed you.'

'Yup, being singled out for repeated searches does that to one,' she said ruefully. He just smiled and photographed the front of the building and got in a couple of shots of the signboards for Apex Imports and the two trusts, very discreet brass-plated affairs.

After checking that the shots were all right they heaved a sigh of relief and decided to take in a sandwich at the local cafe on the way home. As they munched their sandwiches on the train ride back to Bank Station, where Janaki was staying in a business hotel, they decided what to do next.

'It's clear, Uncle, we need to find out the list of donors to the trusts that have paid for the building. We need their annual reports and accounting information, where they list their donors.'

Dave nodded and said that he knew the place to get the information. 'It will take a couple of days, but the annual report should be with my friend Valerie Brown. She coordinates a nodal agency on trusts and has close connections with the registrar's office. All trusts have to declare their donors.'

'Dave Uncle, I don't know what I would have done without you!' said Janaki, for it was an open secret in journalism that most sources were your own family and friends. 'Which is why the rule that we never reveal our sources comes in particularly handy!' Kishoreda used to tell them with a cackle at many editorial meetings.

'That's quite all right, dear; this is a bit of excitement for me as well. Besides, I get to see you after so many years,' he said with a benign smile.

She smiled back, but her fear of what would happen once the story broke kept getting bigger. She had been talking to Vishnu on the phone, but the strain of their last phone conversation always intruded. He had told her that Gayatri was now firmly out of his life, after the ticking off he had given her. Indira Singh had also maintained a diplomatic silence for the last week or so, even been a little subdued.

All this should have pleased Janaki, but it was overshadowed by what she was about to do to Vishnu's boss. Simran had already told her that they were preparing a big splash as far as this story was concerned. 'It will be in three parts. We'll start with the property in London and how foreign trusts have paid for it, and then we will trace the rest of it. Deepak has some stuff on it as well.'

As Janaki got off at her station, and Dave changed for Finchely, she was still mulling over Simran's plan. Which is why, when she came up to street level, she was shocked to bump into Uday.

'Oh! Hi!'

'Hello my dear, nice to see you here,' he said with a smile.

'Uday, how are you? How come you are here?'

'I'm here on holiday, and have some business meetings,' he said vaguely.

Janaki was so stunned to run into Uday that she allowed him to fall in step with her. Before long they stood in front of her hotel. Janaki turned to Uday and said, 'Well, thanks for the escort, but I'm okay now.'

'Nonsense, when two old friends meet in a foreign land, a drink or a meal is mandatory,' he said with a smile.

But Janaki, who was, frankly speaking, feeling fairly put upon by the world, and held Uday solely responsible for the difficult position she found herself in, just frowned at him. 'Uday, I'm sorry, I will have to decline. I have plans with friends—plans I made when I was still in India—so you must excuse me.'

Uday looked a little taken aback. 'Listen, nothing will happen; I won't make a move on you, if that's what you are worried about.'

'Trust me, Uday, that is not what I'm worried about at all.'

'Hey, that's insulting in a way,' he said with a persuasive smile. Janaki was so out of humour with him that she ignored the smile.

'Please, Uday, just let it go.'

'Fine, if that's how you feel. I thought it would make things less awkward between us.'

'We were never thick friends to begin with, so I don't know how you and I not talking would be a problem,' she said crushingly.

Uday took a step back then and gave a smart half-salute. 'Okay then, goodbye Janaki, best of luck.' The last bit of his goodbye struck Janaki as odd and gave her the feeling that he knew what she was doing in London.

~

The next two days flew, but Janaki would have given anything to not know what she knew now. The two trusts that had paid for Apex's offices in London were heavily funded by Blochfeld and Mason, one of the largest aircraft manufacturing companies in the world, and its arms manufacturing unit Bielsen.

While Blochfeld and Mason was bidding heavily for the air force contract, Bielsen was bidding for a missile system to go with it. It was billions of dollars of business; obviously Purushottamam's political muscle was going to be used to swing the deal.

A dejected Janaki was driven to Heathrow airport for her flight back to Delhi. Even as she picked out some chocolates for the office and got a gratifyingly quick upgrade to business class she felt as though she was going to the executioner's block.

Vishnu had been penitent about that evening at his house, and the more he was, the guiltier Janaki felt. She finally decided that she had to give him a clue, albeit one that would not compromise the story. She dialled his number before she lost her nerve. 'Hi!' came his surprised voice down the line.

'Hi Vishnu, I'm at the airport now, ready to board my flight. I . . . I just wanted to tell you that I tried very hard to duck this story, but I had to do it,' she said in a rush.

'Hey, hey, slow down. I'm really not getting what you are saying.'

Janaki took a deep breath and said, 'A story will break on Monday, and it will spell trouble for your boss. Please understand that we had incontrovertible proof of things and that's why the story is running. Try not to hate me, sweetheart.'

'What are you talking about? You don't even cover the ministry of commerce,' he said, sounding perplexed.

'Vishnu, I've already said more than I should. It is kind of unethical of me to have shared this much.'

'I really don't get what you're saying, Janaki. Can't you be straight with me about this? Why the mystery?' he asked, a little exasperated.

'Vishnu, I just want to tell you that this was a professional commitment, but I will understand if you don't want to speak to me after this. I can't say anything more; my flight's just been called.' She hung up the phone.

The past five days in London had possibly been the worst of her life; she didn't like being at odds with Vishnu. Seeing Uday there had sparked off all sorts of suspicions, and also brought home to her the fact that he was never more than an attraction for something untried. It was Vishnu she loved, and now she was going to hurt him. His career would recover; after all, he was completely removed from the deals, but he might not forgive her for keeping all of this a secret for over a month.

The entire eight-hour flight to New Delhi was excruciating for Janaki. No phones, crabby co-passengers and the book she had with her barely held her interest. As she cleared immigration she switched on her phone; she saw there were three missed calls from Vishnu and, surprisingly, one from Saurabh.

She called Saurabh back as soon as she was in the cab. 'Hi, you called?'

'Where have you been?'

'Was out of town. Why?'

'I just wanted to tell you, before you got to know from someone else that Shakira and I are seeing each other. I hope this won't make things awkward for you in office.'

Of all the things Saurabh could have said, this was something she had never expected. 'What? When did this happen?'

'Well, we met up at the ICCR music festival party, and things happened from there.'

Janaki wondered why Saurabh was telling her all this. From where she stood, there could be two reasons for this phone call. Either he wants to make me aware that he has moved on and has a new girl, or he genuinely wants to protect Shakira from an awkward situation at work, she thought. In either case, she was relieved that Saurabh seemed to have moved on. And it was so far away from her problems at the moment that she was tempted to laugh.

'Saurabh, it's quite all right. Don't worry.'

'Are you sure, Janaki?'

'Yeah, yeah, don't worry.'

As the cab made its way out of the congested airport area, she contemplated calling Vishnu back. What will I tell him? I'm in enough trouble already. Either I save my career or my relationship, and since the story will break, I guess my career's a better bet, she thought.

But she couldn't keep away from him; she'd missed him terribly the past five days.

'Hi,' she said, as he answered the phone.

'What the hell did you mean by that phone call, woman?'

'I'm sorry, Vishnu, I can't say more than I already have; you will just have to wait till Monday.'

'You say you're dropping a bomb on me and this is all you give me?'

'Do you know how much trouble I could get into for the stuff that I've told you already?'

'Hang that, you can't play around with my job! Janaki, this is not one of your petty stories, this is the big league!'

Janaki frowned. 'I'm well aware of all that, Vishnu; I cover politics for a living.'

'Yeah, I know all about your job; I deal with your people every day. You'd better tell me.'

'Vishnu, I don't like your tone. What the hell do you mean by running down my job?'

'Look, you people don't run the system. You have no idea what you are getting into! You'd better tell me what this is about.'

'Oh, is that so?' She wasn't surprised by Vishnu's patronizing tone—they had argued about this before. It was one of the things that annoyed her about him; he thought the establishment was everything while she had a more subversive take on things. 'Vishnu, I can't continue this conversation any more. If you think I am such an inconsequential thing, then why are you worried? Enjoy your weekend, or is Gayatri not in town?'

'What the hell do you mean by that?' he asked, his voice rising. Janaki sighed, her temper leaving her in a whoosh. She understood his anger, hell she'd put it there.

'Nothing. I don't mean anything by this. Vishnu, I can't say anything more than this. You have to take me at my word. But it was my job and you are free to deal with it the way you want to.'

Fourteen

For the past four days, Janaki had been hard at work tying up loose ends, filing all three stories of her exposé of the defence deal together so that the newspaper's legal team could go over them and check whether they made any claims without proper evidence to back them up. Simran and Kishoreda had run her ragged. At times she thought Kishoreda was on the verge of a nervous breakdown. 'Just keep the documents in office, and copies with yourself, Janaki, because the government is going to come after us and the truth is our only defence,' he said. Janaki had raised her eyebrows at this dramatic language from Kishoreda, but complied. Of all the different kinds of journalism, investigative journalism was not a favourite.

Janaki would have described herself as a political or even a feature writer, or a reporter who could get a story out of a troubled spot like a riot or a bomb site. 'This is going to surprise a lot of people,' she had confessed to Simran, excitement at breaking a story still overlaying the fear of the consequences.

'Yup, brace yourself,' Simran said.

'What do you mean?'

'You are a woman journalist, breaking a tough story. This is still a testosterone-driven industry, where women are valued as writers or even to project a liberal work atmosphere, but there will be a backlash.'

'What kind?'

'Well, some of your male colleagues will allege that the only way that you, with your female intelligence, could have landed that story would have been by sleeping with some high-up source. After all, ladki ho.

'Some of your own female colleagues will probably join in because they want to be one of the boys, and also resent you for being chosen for this assignment. After all, any one of them could have done the job. As long as you run with the pack it's fine; if you break away from the rest and strike out on your own, then even your own herd will attack you.'

Janaki raised her eyebrows at that.

'Janaki, don't bother about it when it happens. You did a good job of researching the story and Kishoreda is not a fool, he has been training journalists for twenty-seven years, he knows what he is about.'

Janaki smiled, but was disturbed by what she had been told. Simran smiled back at her. 'Chalo, enough serious talk. Please also remember that this story could be the story of your career. Anyway, just tell the page designers that you need to check the graphics on the story.'

~

Even with all that advance warning, Janaki was not prepared for what she faced on Monday. First, the screaming banner headlines: 'Top Minister's Kin in Kickback Scandal' ran the eight column spread. A picture of Purushottamam and his brother along with a graphic detailing the money trail lay below.

Janaki's phone was ringing off the hook all morning, with her friends congratulating her on the big breaking story. Television channel editors were ambushed with the headlines in the morning and now had stationed crews outside Purushottamam's official residence. It was said that the man himself was in Madurai. The one phone call that Janaki was dreading and longing for at the same time did not come. Vishnu hadn't called, and it seemed as though they were over.

Janaki called up Simran and said that television channels had asked her to give them some of the incriminating papers to take the story forward and build a campaign to oust Purushottamam. While stories were broken all the time, this was being touted as India's next Bofors scandal—something that could shake the government—and everyone wanted in on the action. Simran counselled patience. 'Let all three parts appear. We have to establish that this is not a tenuous connection we are drawing; this allegation in the paper is backed up by documents, the government's own agencies' tax notices to the companies, and the property in London. We have to have undisputed ownership of the story, then let the mudslide begin.'

Janaki nodded. Her paperwork had been thorough—she had no doubts about that.

~

Janaki's phone rang. It was a central Delhi landline number. 'Hello?' she said cautiously.

'What the hell made you do this?' Vishnu asked, his voice cold and angry.

'Vishnu, this is what I do for a living, and I warned you too.'

'Warned me? Do you know how this will look? I was the one who introduced you to Purushottamam; now not only will he be furious, he will think I put you up to it!'

'That's rubbish. I barely met the man once! And he is an arms dealer, Vishnu, why the hell would you want the good opinion of a man like that?'

'It's not a question of good opinion, you stupid woman; the first thing anyone looks for in any kind of key appointment is loyalty! My involvement with you and your involvement with this story means that I cannot be trusted.'

Vishnu had received a disturbing call from Venkataraman. 'My boy, you are in for it for the next few days at least. And this girl's name is familiar, isn't she the one who was in Madurai during the blast?'

'Yes sir.'

'That is bad news if it gets out. Your loyalty would be called into question, and you know how the political class is, completely suspicious.'

Vishnu was aware of the fragile trust between a bureaucrat and a politician, and knew the disastrous consequences for his career. It wasn't that he would be called upon to be corrupt, only to turn a blind eye to certain things. Fortunately, Vishnu had worked for honest bosses—this was his first experience of anything like this. His thoughts returned to the present with a thud. 'Didn't you think for once what this would do to me?'

'Vishnu, that is the only thing that is stopping me from actually enjoying the fact that I have exposed a corrupt man!'

'Oh, come off your pulpit, Janaki, I thought you lived in the real world.'

'I do live in the real world, Vishnu, which is why I want you to get out from in front of the mirror and break out of your self-absorption. This isn't about you or me; it's about a story and some corruption. You were just an innocent bystander.'

'How am I just an innocent bystander when this directly affects me?'

'Hello! This doesn't concern you, Vishnu, it concerns your boss, whose family is selling the country down the river! Unless of course you were in on this,' she said now quite angry.

'Just shut up,' he said, incensed.

'You shut up and get your head out of your ass! This is a news story; it's huge and if you have nothing to do with it, you have nothing to worry about. You are a bureaucrat, you will get another posting.'

'Stop this patronizing drivel!'

'There is one way of ensuring that, just hang up,' she dared him. He took her dare and as Janaki heard him disconnect, she was moved to tears. I've screwed it up royally this time, she said to herself. But Janaki felt that there was nothing different she could have said. Granted, this would affect Vishnu's job but, as an upright class I officer, there was nothing much anybody could do to him to really hurt his career.

They had kept their relationship hush-hush, and now there no longer was any question that it would go anywhere, she told herself in an orgy of misery. She decided that she might as well enjoy the glory of having broken the story and leave for the office.

~

As she entered the office a couple of her colleagues congratulated her, but it was Monika who told her something that completely ruined her day. 'Listen, apparently Vishnu spoke to Shakira, and has been quite vocal about his anger at the story. He let it slip that you had warned him about it as well.'

Janaki's heart sank. 'Hmmm,' she said, as she saw Simran waving at her, pointing to her cabin. Quite clearly she had heard Shakira's little snippet.

Simran shot Janaki a questioning look. 'Janaki, what's this I'm hearing? You told Purushottamam's private secretary that this would happen?'

Janaki took a deep breath and decided to come clean. 'Simran, Vishnu and I have been dating for a while now. It began when I met him in Chennai.'

Simran raised her hand and asked her to halt her explanation. 'All that is just by the way. Did you tell him that this story was going to come out?'

Janaki cast her eyes down. 'I told him that something was going to put his boss in a spot. I didn't discuss any details or anything. He didn't know anything till Thursday morning.'

Simran rubbed her eyes. 'Janaki, you have crossed a major line. You should not have done that; you compromised the paper. People get sacked for less!'

Janaki did not know how to reply to that. 'But he hasn't told Purushottamam anything, I'm sure of that.'

'That was not his call to make, Janaki, and you have not done the right thing. Kishoreda requires an explanation. Fortunately, you have done a good job on the story, and it's getting the attention it's supposed to get. Hear him out, give him a written apology—and no cute answers, Janaki; it was a mistake; be penitent. I'll talk to him and ask him to let it go at that.'

Janaki nodded.

'What I want to know is what prompted him to tell Shakira,' said Simran, putting her finger on just what was bugging the hell out of Janaki as well.

'We fought this morning. He was upset that I didn't tell him sooner and didn't divulge the details.'

'Hmmm, probably thinks his job is more important than yours,' said Simran laconically.

Janaki shrugged.

'Occupational hazard when it comes to men, especially establishment stooges. Anyway, go make amends with Kishoreda, and send Shakira in on your way out.'

Janaki walked out of Simran's cabin with a heavy tread. She called out to Shakira, and knocked on Kishoreda's cabin. Kishoreda looked at her over his spectacles and waved her to a chair. 'This is not done, Janaki; you endangered the whole campaign with your indiscretion.'

Janaki nodded mutely; she really had nothing to say.

'You have broken rules all over the place. The story may be yours but it is the property of the paper.'

Again Janaki had nothing to say, her misery at being hauled up like this swamped by anger at Vishnu. *If he wanted to avenge himself on me he couldn't have done it better,* she thought.

'I suppose Simran has told you that people have been sacked for less.'

Janaki nodded.

'I want a written apology, Janaki; you are lucky that it didn't actually compromise the story!'

'Yes sir,' she said. Her walk of shame back to her desk did nothing to detract from her realization that she had no boyfriend and no glory either. As she switched on her computer to send the apology mail, she saw a broadcast message from the editor. It mentioned that the newspaper had come across 'an instance of stories being discussed with people not authorized to know about them'. It went on to detail the code of ethics required of reporters. Quite obviously the office was taking things very seriously.

Janaki typed out her letter of apology and decided that she wouldn't let anyone put her in this position again. She felt humiliated and, worst of all, she had lost on both fronts. Either I should have come clean with Vishnu, or kept completely mum, she thought. Now I have just capsized both boats.

She opened the file on the second part of the story; the desk had sent it back with some queries and she had to approve the final version that was going to be printed. Her painstaking research into Apex's accounts seemed to mock her in her miserable state of mind. She had always known she would be torn up over the story, but this was awful.

She felt a hand on her shoulder, and turned around to see Deepak. 'Hi,' he said. Janaki nodded in reply.

'Teri story maine dekh li hai, it's fine.'

Janaki gave him a wan smile.

'Sun, what are you doing in the evening?'

'Kuch nahin, yaar; I guess I'll go home.'

'You've broken the story of the year and you're still being kanjoos! Koi baat nahin, I'll treat you to a drink. Be ready at seven, we'll head out to FCC.'

The Foreign Correspondents Club (FCC), set up by overseas correspondents in India, was a cosy watering hole and had more Indian journalists as members now.

Janaki smiled at him, grateful for his attempts to cheer her up. 'Thanks, Deepak, chalenge.'

'That's my girl!'

~

They walked into the FCC and immediately spotted a couple of people from the *Daily Hindustan* nursing beers and talking in the hyperbolic way of all journalists. 'Bas, yeh log aaj sarkar gira hi denge,' whispered Deepak to Janaki, a reference to a claim by most journalists in their cups.

Janaki giggled at that, and waved to the two. Deepak and she had just ordered their beers when Deepak suddenly turned serious. 'Janaki, I have known Vishnu for a long time, he's not the type who would snitch like this, and he doesn't even like Shakira. There is something else to this.'

'I don't know what it could be, Deepak. We had a huge fight in the morning and he accused me of screwing up his career.'

Deepak sighed. 'Look, he's in the government; wahan par you are as good as your discretion. If it gets out that he knew you, it will raise all sorts of questions about his role in the entire thing.'

'I know all that, Deepak, and I warned him about it. What I want to know is why would he want Shakira to know that I told him. After this we were over anyway, so no one would have known in any case.'

'That is true. Something doesn't add up.'

They discussed the matter for some time after that, exploring every possible angle to the story when Deepak finally said, 'Listen, I think I really need to talk to him about it.'

'No, please don't. It won't serve any purpose.'

'For my own satisfaction, Janaki, after all, I introduced you to him,' he said with a smile. Janaki gave a bittersweet smile in return.

Fifteen

The next few days passed as if in a dream. Purushottamam was summoned to Chennai by his party high command. He tried to stay defiant in the face of the opposition demanding his resignation. He alleged that he was a victim of a political conspiracy. Janaki, who felt no joy at this man's discomfort, knew that it wasn't far from the truth. We were given the papers by the opposition, she said to herself.

When she was growing up, her dream was to be a known journalist travelling the world, penning stories. Now, when she was at the centre of the biggest political storm in India in recent years, the sense of achievement she thought she would feel was nowhere to be found.

She rebooted her computer to put out what she considered her daily log—her email to Dave Houghton to keep him updated on the storm they had unleashed. She hadn't spoken to or seen Vishnu since the day the story broke. Come to think of it, she hadn't seen Uday Pratap either.

Guys suck, she thought to herself. One was around till his work was done, the other thinks he is the centre of the universe!

The word on the street was that Purushottamam would resign before the next session of Parliament. The next morning Janaki went off to South Block. Purushottamam wanted to resign in one final burst of media glory or infamy and have his fifteen seconds of fame before investigative agencies swooped down on him. His defiance in the face of the media campaign against him was typical of the pugnacious minister, and a reflection of the fact that nobody had really ever been convicted for corruption in the country until now. Cases dragged on for years, public memory was short; why admit guilt or shame when a court case could outlast your political career?

Purushottamam's meeting with the prime minister was scheduled for 11 a.m.; he wanted to go down in a blaze of glory. Despite wanting to avoid Purushottamam, Janaki was told to cover this assignment.

'You started it; you finish up,' Simran said. Sympathy for Janaki had been in short supply in the office lately, especially with Simran. There were too many early morning assignments being thrown her way, stuff that was usually doled out to trainees.

It was well into winter in Delhi and Janaki pulled her jacket closer to herself as she stood outside the Prime Minister's Office at South Block, a steel barrier between her and the portico where Purushottamam would alight. Several camera crews had already made themselves comfortable near the barrier.

'Fantastic story, Janaki,' Ashish Dua, correspondent for World Wide Television, said as they waited in the draughty morning.

'Thanks,' said Janaki, without her heart in it; she felt no joy at the story. 'Come here to see it through to the end, have you?' he asked her.

'Yup,' she said laconically. The end is right, she thought miserably to herself, casting her mind back to Chennai, where she had met Vishnu for the first time, and their time together in Delhi. She snapped out of her reverie when Purushottamam drew up at the PMO's portico in his red-topped ambassador car. Cameras whirred as he got out, pulled his shawl close to his shoulders—despite the cold he was wearing the regulation white veshti and shirt, albeit with socks and sandals. He turned to the waiting cameras, 'I will give a byte when I return,' he said.

He was gone for fifteen minutes, after which he came out and waited on the other side of the steel barriers for the television mikes to be fixed in position. When all was set, he said, 'As of this moment I have resigned from the Union cabinet. My resignation is not an admission of guilt. I insist that I have been framed and I promise my people, those who voted for me, that I shall get to the bottom of this conspiracy. I have resigned to make sure that our government can be fearless and above all suspicion in the investigation.' Essentially, he made the statement that every politician made when caught with a hand in the till.

As he turned to leave his gaze fell on Janaki, who was hanging around behind the cameras. 'Madam, I would like a word with you, please,' he said to her. Janaki was taken aback but went up to the barrier where he stood. Fortunately nobody had heard him and most of the media was busy packing up equipment.

'Madam, you have been used to get me out. Hear me out. My rival, Mudaliar, will be getting this portfolio now, and the man who had given you the documents will make the most of that appointment.'

Janaki frowned, a little puzzled.

'If you don't believe me, just watch and wait.'

Janaki didn't say a word. Her discomfort with taking the papers from Uday Pratap returned in a rush, along with the feeling that she had barely cracked the surface of this conundrum. She stared steadily back at Purushottamam, her gaze unwavering. He gave her a mocking smile and got back into his car. He knew he'd got a burr under her saddle.

~

Janaki was still mulling over Purushottamam's words as she headed back to her office. She filed a colour copy on his resignation and the fact that Mudaliar of the opposite faction in the party would be his successor in the commerce ministry. As she crosschecked the facts and sent her copy off to the desk, Monika walked by. 'Er, Mon, can you just step out with me for some tea?'

'Sure,' said Monika, and they both headed to a tea stall outside the office. Despite the tea and coffee dispenser, the old-fashioned tea stall was a real favourite.

'Haan, tell me what happened. Vishnu in touch again?'

Janaki shook her head. 'That won't happen; don't hold your breath. I'm worried about something Purushottamam said today. He said that the chap who gave us the documents had an interest in getting him out of this particular ministry and that there was a deal between this guy and Mudaliar, the new commerce minister.'

'Boss, you're talking in riddles. Please remember I don't know who gave you those papers.'

Janaki shook her head. 'I'll tell you all that, but I need you to find out something for me.'

'Haan, bol.'

'Can you find out from your sources about (a) whether the NRP MP Uday Pratap has anything to do with export–import and stuff, and (b) if there was any particular policy decision affecting imports or exports that Purushottamam had been blocking.'

Monika nodded her head, frowning. 'Um, you do one thing. Get Uday Pratap's list of assets and liabilities from the Election Commission. Let's see whether he is listed as a director or something in any company, and then let's take it from there.'

Janaki nodded. 'That's fine, but what I think I should do is get hold of one of his rivals in the party and get some dope on the guy. There is something here that doesn't add up Monika.'

'Fine, that also appears okay. But I thought you liked him.'

Janaki gave her a wan smile. 'I have always felt that I was being made a patsy in this situation, maybe not by the office, but by those interested in seeing the story in print. I want to know. I can't be Alice in Wonderland any more and believe in the altruism of this story.'

Monika looked at Janaki. 'You're really serious about it, aren't you?'

Janaki looked back at her steadily. 'This story has effectively ruined my relationship with the man I love. Someone has to feel the pain of it; it can't all be for me.'

'Dekh, I'll get you the information, but just be careful.'

'Yeah, yeah,' Janaki replied.

~

Vishnu drove down to his office at Udyog Bhawan, his mind in turmoil. Janaki's story had certainly changed his circumstances. Purushottamam, never one to miss a trick, had summoned him to his house two days after the story broke. 'Singh, isn't this one of the people you introduced me to?'

'Yes sir,' Vishnu replied, staring steadily back at the man.

'Hmm . . . did you know, I have been racking my brains thinking about why this paper would suddenly get after me. I know I have enemies in Chennai, but not how they managed to breach this newspaper.'

Vishnu didn't know how that was in any way concerned with him, so he kept silent.

'Don't worry, I know you didn't have anything to do with this Singh, but tell this girl, if you meet her, that the people who got me out are no better,' he said with a snort. 'You do know that Mudaliar will take over this portfolio?'

Vishnu shook his head. 'I didn't know.'

'Anna told me in Chennai. Anyway, let's see how far this goes.' Purushottamam dismissed Vishnu, who didn't know quite what to say to the disgraced leader. The accusations were fairly fierce, but Vishnu understood what Purushottamam had been trying to tell him, that there were wheels within wheels.

Deep in thought, Vishnu returned to his office to pack up his things; he had been told that he could proceed on leave till it was decided what to do with the rest of his central deputation. He was just packing up some books that he kept in his office when his phone rang.

It was Indira Singh. 'Beta, you left home quite early, I wanted to talk to you a bit,' she started.

'Kya baat hai, Ma?' he asked her. Communication between

them had been reduced to a bare minimum after that horrible dinner a few weeks ago. It seemed like an age had passed since then, and a pang of longing shot through Vishnu as he thought of Janaki. Despite the way their last conversation had gone, he missed her like hell.

'Beta, I've come to know that that girl you introduced me to is the one responsible for your central deputation coming to an end.'

Vishnu sighed and, not for the first time, wished his father was alive. 'Ma, my boss was found indulging in corruption of the worst kind, which is why he lost his job and I have to wait for a new posting.'

'Woh toh sabhi kartey hain; she should not have done this to you. I knew she would not make a good wife for you!'

At this Vishnu saw red. 'Ma, please, for the last time, don't interfere in things you know nothing about. For your information, that girl as you call her, put her job on the line to warn me that this was going to happen. Frankly, I don't think I would have done the same in her position!'

'Nonsense! Why should you? You are in the government; in journalists ka kya hai,' his mother promptly replied.

'Ma, I don't want to discuss this. You have made your opinion clear, and I have made mine. Let's leave it at that. I have to pack up my things, I'll be a little late coming home,' he said and hung up the phone.

'Hi Vishnu,' came a familiar voice from the door of his office. He turned to see Shakira Banerjee swing her way into his office. God, this is all I need, he thought to himself. 'Shakira, please, I'm a little busy. You will have to excuse me.'

'Never mind, Vishnu, I'll leave. I just dropped in to say hi. Best of luck with everything!' Just as suddenly as she had appeared, she left, leaving Vishnu a little bemused but relieved as hell.

The conversation with his mother had left a bad taste in his mouth. Until he told off his mother he hadn't acknowledged to himself just what Janaki had risked in calling him up and warning him. And what did you tell her in return? That her job wasn't worth squat and that all that mattered was you and your worthless career, he thought to himself.

Vishnu felt a dull pain in his gut as he realized that he had probably lost the one woman who meant the world to him, all over one corrupt man and the prospect of an uncomfortable posting. He boxed the rest of his books and told the peon to load the stuff in his car. The peon just stared dumbly at him, shaking his head.

'Now what?' Vishnu asked.

'Sir, CBI aayegi, kaha gaya hai ki kuch samaan baahar nahin jaayega.'

Jeepers, what the hell will they find here, Vishnu thought to himself. He shrugged; it was just a bunch of annual reports anyway, just something he wanted from his stint in Delhi, which, despite its ignominious end, was one of the happiest periods in his life. And now I've gone and royally screwed it up, he thought to himself.

Sixteen

A month went by and the spotlight on the scam faded. As was typical with media storms not backed up by enough legal action, Janaki's life too slowly limped back to normal. Her routine went back to the way it had been before the exposé: the morning newspaper scan, phone calls to sources, a round of the NRP party office, going to her own office, filing stories and going home.

She had pretty much withdrawn into herself after the Apex stories had come out. She missed Vishnu, but burned up with anger every time she thought of him snitching her out to Shakira.

As she looked at her buxom colleague, she wondered how Saurabh could be with her after being with Janaki, seeing that they were miles apart in personality. Maybe that's the draw, Janaki thought desultorily. In any case, she was glad that one thing had come out of the whole thing—the fact that she and Saurabh were just not suited to each other. Janaki decided that now was as good a time as any to go home to her mother.

'Simran, could you please sign my leave application?' Relations between them were still not on an even keel, but Janaki felt she deserved a holiday whether Simran was inclined to grant it or not.

Simran looked up from her computer. 'Leave? When are you planning to take leave?'

'Next week. I want to visit my mother; it's been nearly a year since I saw her last.'

Simran looked back at her steadily, and suddenly smiled. 'Fine, I think I've been more than tough on you these past few weeks,' she said and signed the form.

Janaki didn't smile back; she just took the form and turned to leave.

'Janaki, wait. What's the matter? Are you upset about something?'

Janaki sighed and said, 'Simran, I really don't want to discuss it.'

Simran was not having any of it. 'Stop right there. You will bloody well discuss it with me.'

Janaki turned around and without a preamble spoke. 'The story was good, but I had reservations about the source of the papers and continue to have them. I don't like being made a patsy, Simran. I want to know why I was picked for this story. Deepak could have done just as well.'

Simran looked back at her. 'Janaki, I had this conversation with Kishoreda. He told me that it was an editorial decision that someone not covering either the commerce or the defence ministry should do the story. You had a background in business reporting; you were picked. Plus, Uday also said he was comfortable with you.'

The last bit startled Janaki.

'Uday Pratap? He didn't even know me before you sent me to meet him. I had only bumped into him in Parliament. Why would he specify that he wanted me? And since when does Kishoreda listen to anyone when it comes to editorial decisions?' she asked, now a little belligerent.

'Calm down, Janaki; it wasn't like that. He'd told us he had something interesting. We were just talking of the kind of reporter who should break the story, and somehow, during that discussion, the choice centred on you. There was no agenda, believe me.'

Janaki looked at Simran pityingly. 'Simran, I want your word on something.' Simran looked at her enquiringly. 'If I get something on Uday Pratap, you have to let me run it.'

Simran raised her eyebrows at that. 'Something on Uday Pratap? Sure. Why do you need to ask?'

'Because it seems you and Kishoreda hold him in high esteem, from the way that you didn't question the papers he gave you, or his motives for giving them to you.'

Simran shrugged and said, 'When you've spent as long as I have in journalism you get used to stories coming in from the unlikeliest of sources.'

Janaki just nodded and let it go. 'Fine, I have your word then,' she said and walked out of the cabin.

Seventeen

Janaki breathed in the nippy Bangalore air and lay back on her couch. She was home, curled up with a book, good old coconut oil in her hair. This vacation was going very well indeed. Despite all the heartbreak in Delhi, Janaki was happy to see her mother; her calm routine had soothed her into an umbilical state from which she didn't want to emerge.

Mythili bustled into her room with some coffee in her hand. 'Janaki, you've spent the entire day indoors; just get out and get some fresh air!' she said imperiously.

Janaki took the coffee and wailed, 'But Amma, I will have to wash my hair; just let me be.'

Mythili set down the cup. 'Your excuses are not going to work any more young lady; you will wash your hair and come with me to Lila chikamma's house for the haldi kumkum pooje.'

Janaki groaned. Though she liked her aunt, she didn't want to meet all the neighbourhood aunties, who would invariably pester her about marriage. 'Amma, please, you know I don't want to face all those aunties; they will ask the same things, "When are you getting married?" "When will you have babies?" Ugh!'

Mythili smiled. Sitting down next to her only child, she couldn't quite keep the concern out of her eyes. 'Janaki, there is something else at work here, isn't it? What happened between you and Saurabh? Did he misbehave with you?' she asked softly.

'No, Amma, nothing like that.'

'Then? Sweetheart, just tell me, I worry.'

Janaki felt ashamed of herself for moping around her mother's house like this. 'Amma, the reason I broke up with Saurabh was because I met someone else. You remember I went to Chennai to cover the assembly elections? I met Vishnu there.'

Her mother raised her eyebrows. 'Hmm, who is this man? And how far has this gone?'

Janaki told her mother about Vishnu and her, leaving out the slightly risqué bits of course, and certainly every mention of Uday Pratap. It was, however, when she spoke to her mother about her meeting with Indira Singh that Mythili lost her cool. 'Janaki, I'm ashamed of you! You met his mother, played the coy daughter-in-law-to-be and didn't even tell me all this was happening?'

Janaki felt really ashamed.

'You want to behave like an orphan? People will kick you around!' Mythili said in a huff.

'Amma, I'm sorry, but please listen to the rest of it as well,' Janaki begged. As she told her mother the rest of the story, Janaki realized the truth of what her mother was saying. She should have stood up for herself, and if Vishnu had wanted to take their relationship to the next level then her mother should also have been included in the family introductions.

'Amma, you are right. I will never allow this to happen again.'

Mythili looked sternly at her and said, 'All that is fine, but now that you have fought with the boy, what do you plan to do?'

'I don't know what to do. I'm following the lead Purushottamam gave me; if I have been made a stool pigeon, I'm going to find out why and expose it,' she said with quiet determination.

Mythili just looked at her and asked, 'Janaki, I have never stopped you from following your heart in whatever you do, and that is probably one of the reasons why you are in this situation. You allowed these people to walk all over you.'

Janaki just lowered her gaze, feeling quite ashamed. 'You did stand up for yourself in the end; what I want to know is why you allowed it to go so far. As far as I can see, you should have told

Simran you were dating this boy. If he was that important to you, you should have gotten out of the story. You let the situation dangle and compromised your ethics.'

Janaki felt more and more miserable as her mother told her off.

'Career is important, so is having a personal life, but it won't work without being honest to both. You were honest to neither and that's why this has happened. The boy is a bit self-important, but then all men are. You ambushed him and, like a spoilt brat, wanted him to fall in line,' she added, now on a roll.

'And that mother of his! Let me at her! I'll fix her!'

Janaki just burst out laughing. 'Oh Amma, you're fierce, dude! I'll marry Vishnu just to see you bring down that woman a peg or two.'

Mythili smiled and relaxed a bit. 'Now, as punishment, you have to come with me to Lila chikamma's house. Get ready, wear a nice sari and put on a bindi—you look nice with it.'

~

Janaki came back from her vacation charged up and bathed in the glow of maternal love. It was Kajal's birthday the weekend she returned, and an outing with her old friends did much to reinforce the benefits of her vacation.

It had now been quite a while since the Apex scam and things at work too had become normal. Shakira and Janaki hadn't spoken since the day Shakira had snitched and quietly ignored each other at work. The budget session of Parliament was about to start, and Simran wanted to know the opposition's plans to corner the government, since it would be the first session since the Apex scam broke. As Purushottamam had predicted, V. Mudaliar had taken his portfolio and been sworn in as Union commerce minister. Janaki remembered her vow and had put in a Right to Information request at the commerce ministry about some policy issues on which letters had been received from MPs, lobbying for any particular slant. She hit pay dirt as the Election Commission's information revealed that Uday Pratap's wife Vaishali Singh was on the board of Shanti Exports, a commodities export company, mainly into exporting wheat and rice, opening a whole new dimension to everything.

'If there are any moves by the opposition, both Left and Right, to band together and mount an attack on the government, that would be big—the general elections are just a year and a half away, so this should help.'

Janaki came back to earth with a thud as Simran briefed them on the upcoming Parliament session. And while Janaki was happy to be back at work, she was a lot more detached from it. The wonder had gone out of it, she felt. Perhaps because of the fact that she hadn't spoken to Vishnu since the fight they had had, or perhaps because she had found her professional world shallow and its victories without glory. Janaki decided that work would be just that—work.

As she trudged into Parliament, she recalled the day she had met Vishnu there: the heat of his gaze, the pounding of her heart and her shy confession to Monika, about that sweet first kiss.

She wondered where he was and, as always, there was a pang in her heart and her stomach contracted thinking of him. I was just a fool, first to fall for him and then to get confused and lose him for good. I could have been gentler, she kept telling herself. Her dalliance with Uday Pratap appeared so futile and foolish in comparison that she wondered why she had ever bothered. It is done, however, and we must move on—she tried to put a brave face on things.

Janaki was stopped on her way inside by Nityanand Kumar, minister for roads, known to be a ladies' man, quite mistakenly believing that it was because of his looks. Janaki and most women journalists avoided him like the plague.

'Hi Janaki, been making waves, I see. Should I be afraid?' he asked, leering.

'I don't know, sir, do you have anything to be afraid of?' she returned with a smile. With Nityanand it was always better to banter and run. 'Now if political reporters start doing investigative stories, then we have to be afraid,' he said with a laugh and the coterie of male journalists around him laughed with him.

'Dekhiye, ab hamara chehra dekh kar toh story thodi koi dega, sir,' said Shailender Singh, a reporter with *Samaj Nirman*; the rest of the group grinned knowingly at that.

Janaki was quite used to these chauvinistic comments but decided to answer in their own coin. 'Now, now, Shailender, don't worry, here comes Vanaja Shastri, women and child development minister, I'm sure she has a global scoop for you,' she said with a sickeningly sweet smile.

The barb hit its mark and Shailender actually had the grace to blush. Janaki softened her smile and said, 'Why are you teaming up with the enemy? You are from our biraadari,' she said and walked off.

This was not the first barb she would face and certainly not the last. But she was on a mission today, to corner Rajeev Verma, a Joint Secretary in the commerce ministry who was privy to the tussles in the ministry over a proposed change in the export policy for wheat.

She waited outside the gallery leading up to the central hall of Parliament. Senior journalists with more than ten years of parliamentary coverage were allowed inside the central hall, which functioned as a sort of canteen for MPs on ordinary days, but Janaki hadn't made the grade yet.

As she waited, she could see Rajeev Verma come out of the central hall, and walk towards her. 'Sir, could I have a minute with you?'

'Sorry, I'm in a bit of a rush.'

'Sir, I just wanted to know on what grounds an export ban on a certain commodity is waived.'

He stopped and turned and looked at Janaki.

'Aren't you Janaki Rao?'

'Yes sir.'

'Well, my dear, it is more than my job is worth to tell you that, but since I thoroughly enjoyed your reporting in December, I will tell you anyway. You can ask for a waiver on the ban on export only if you are exporting wheat or rice or any cereal for humanitarian purposes.'

'And sir, has any such waiver been asked for in the past, and granted,' she asked almost diffidently. She knew Rajeev Verma was one of those upright officers who quietly let out stories that exposed the misdeeds of colleagues.

'Why yes, a waiver for a huge consignment of wheat to Nigeria was asked for. It was stopped during the previous minister's tenure and has recently been granted. As to the rest, I suggest you resort to that wonderful thing called RTI,' he said with a twinkle in his eye.

Janaki smiled back; now she knew her RTI query had been forwarded to Verma himself. With a smart salute, she spun around and almost ran out of the gallery. As she turned the corner she collided with Uday Pratap.

'Oh oh, steady on,' he said and when he saw it was Janaki, impervious to the watch and watch staff of Parliament he said, 'See? The fates want you in my arms, Janaki; stop fighting it!'

Janaki stepped back. 'Like flies to wanton boys are we to the gods, they kill us for their sport,' she quoted Hamlet back at him. 'Fight what the gods have in store, sir; I don't believe in accepting my fate,' she said, looking meaningfully at him.

He frowned. 'Now why does that give me the feeling that you mean to say quite something else?' Janaki stared at his face and, probably because of her building prejudice against him, detected a smug satisfaction lurking there. 'You can think whatever you want,' she said and flounced off.

~

Janaki typed out her copy and double-checked the dates on the documents she had spread before her. The RTI replies had come in thick and fast that week, and confirmed that Shanti Exports, with Vaishali Singh as a board member, had petitioned the commerce ministry for an exemption on the ban on the export of wheat, which was in place because wheat prices in India had risen. Purushottamam had decided not to grant the exemption. Now, of course, Mudaliar had given the company a dispensation to export to Nigeria on humanitarian grounds, because of a purported famine there.

Janaki had already got a letter from the Nigerian embassy in Delhi on behalf of their government stating that there was, in fact, no official famine in the country. So, the assumption was that Rs 650 crore worth of wheat had made its way to another country under false pretences. As she sent her copy off to Simran to be vetted, Janaki hoped and prayed that the story would be listed for page 1. She wanted to knock Uday Pratap's socks off. Thinks I'm a soft touch, does he? she said vengefully to herself.

Simran rang for Janaki, who promptly went to her cabin.

'Yes, Simran?'

'Janaki, this is a cracker of a story. I want to know who told you all this.'

'I got all the documents using RTI, Simran, nobody planted this on me. I worked on a tip-off—it's a genuine scoop.'

'Hmm, so this is what you meant by some dirt on Uday Pratap Singh. I'll have to run it by Kishoreda.'

'Do,' said Janaki, raising an eyebrow. She had hoped her diligent paperwork would have got the copy cleared in a jiffy; it seemed that she had been wrong.

'Simran, you promised,' she said to her boss, now quite fearless.

'That I did,' Simran admitted. 'Theek hai, let's run with it. Kishoreda is on leave; we'll see tomorrow if there is a reaction.'

Janaki left the cabin with a light heart. Now we shall see, she said to herself.

~

The next morning her phone rang shrilly at 7.30 a.m. It was Uday Pratap, and Janaki was more than prepared for the call. 'You stupid cow, what the hell do you think you are playing at?' came a very belligerent voice on the phone.

'Hello Udayji,' said Janaki, calmly and coldly.

'What in the world do you think you would gain by this shit? And here I was wooing you! Christ! How could you?'

'How could you? You used me to get one minister out and get another in, just so your export order goes through?'

'I gave you the story of your life!'

'Oh get off your high horse, Uday! What if Purushottamam had cleared your order; would it have mattered to you who got the defence deal? As for my career, don't bother doing me any favours.'

'How the hell do you think other journalists get stories? You think you are above these things?'

'I don't care how others get them; I don't like being used. And hell yes, I *am* above these things. If that means I can't be a journalist, then see if I give a rat's ass about it!'

'After all we meant to each other, you did this to me . . .' he changed tack seeing that things were getting a bit out of hand.

'What did we mean to each other, Uday? Stop being such a girl about one little kiss,' she said viciously.

'My god, you are a cold bitch, and that sucker who went back to Chennai with his tail between his legs deserves you!'

One more piece of the puzzle fell into place. She had been picked for the story just because she had been seeing Vishnu. Her secret love was known to this man, and suddenly she felt dirty, as though Uday had watched Vishnu and her in bed or something.

'So you knew?'

'Yeah, I knew; we had been watching Purushottamam's staff for some time. And I knew that it would be easy for people to believe you were given the story by your boyfriend, and nobody would be able to trace it to me.'

'I have nothing more to say, Uday.'

'Oh this isn't over by a long shot yet, Janaki.'

'You don't scare me; you never did,' she said and hung up the phone.

The encounter had left her drained. Uday Pratap's revelation that he had known about her and Vishnu and had therefore specifically asked for her as the reporter on the story had stunned her. She felt exposed and dirty, and repeatedly castigated herself for ever having kissed Uday Pratap.

There was another niggling doubt in her mind though: Kishoreda. How could he have allowed himself to be led to the trough like that? It was his prerogative to assign a story to a reporter. Why had he fallen in line with Uday Pratap's wishes?

Just then an SMS beeped on her phone. It was Simran, asking her to get to the office fast. It was just 8 a.m., but it already looked like it would be a very long day.

~

It was still very early when she entered the office, typically deserted at that time. She walked up to Simran's cabin, surprisingly unconcerned by whatever it was that was about to happen. Already TV cameras were outside Uday Pratap's house, following this latest scam. His detractors within the party were giving out sanctimonious TV sound bites about the impropriety of such scams and the need for honesty in public life.

Janaki had wreaked some revenge, and felt contented. Simran looked up when Janaki entered her cabin. 'Sit, Janaki; Kishoreda will be here in some time. He wants to see you about your story today. By the way, Uday Pratap called me this morning; he was angry to say the least.'

Janaki nodded. 'Yeah, he called me too.'

'Hmm, it's okay.' Janaki smiled. Simran, at least, was the way she was supposed to be.

Janaki looked steadily at Simran and said, 'By the way, I was requested as a reporter for the story because Vishnu and I were seeing each other.'

'Who told you that?' Simran asked her, a little surprised.

'Uday Pratap told me quite explicitly. He was really pissed off and blurted it all out.'

Simran raised her eyebrows. 'Janaki, sometimes it's better to take a view from 30,000 feet above the ground,' she said cryptically.

'What?'

'Kishoreda is the editor of the paper, and works under many pulls and pressures. Don't be upset and, for heaven's sake, don't do anything precipitate.'

As they both asked for some coffee and sat sipping it, Janaki pondered over what Simran had said. 'There are pitfalls in every job, Janaki. I grant that in our profession, the hours are crappy and the pay is even worse. But we do get to do pretty much what we want most of the time. You did one story you did not agree with, but look at the many stories you did out of a sheer sense of conviction.'

Janaki nodded. 'Simran, I agree with all that, but I want to know just what drove Kishoreda to do this.'

'Well, we are about to find out,' she said as her phone rang, summoning the two of them to Kishoreda's office.

The man himself was going through Janaki's story as they entered the office, and he waved them to a couple of chairs in front of his desk.

'Janaki, who gave you this tip-off?' Kishoreda asked her as soon as they were seated.

'Sir, Purushottamam, the day he quit as minister,' she replied calmly.

'Do you know how much trouble I've got into from the management over the story?'

'No sir, I don't see how a factually correct story with verifiable sourcing can get any journalist into trouble.'

'Don't be facetious, Janaki,' he growled. 'Anyway, the damage has been done. I suggest you take a leave of absence for some time, and wait for the fuss to die down.'

'But why . . .?' Janaki started to ask, when she felt a kick on her shin.

Simran looked at her and motioned for her to keep silent. 'Fine,' Janaki said, and she and Simran got up to leave. As they filed out of

Kishoreda's office, Simran held Janaki's arm and almost forced her towards her own cabin.

'Janaki, now, don't do anything foolish. Believe me when I tell you, Kishoreda is probably saving your job. Just go on leave for a couple of weeks.'

Janaki simply nodded and went back to her workstation. Fortunately it was early still for anyone from her department to have come to the office. She picked up her handbag and car keys, and walked out of the office, her heart quite light. Why, I may not even decide to return after two weeks, she thought to herself.

For the first time in six years, she had two weeks of leave stretching before her with no deadlines, no sources to meet and no idea what to do. Janaki went home, leaving a goggle-eyed Mrs Mishra in her wake, astounded to see Janaki around at this hour, and went straight to bed.

~

It was eight in the evening when Janaki woke up, to the shrill ringing of her phone. It was Deepak. 'Where the hell have you been? I've been worried sick ever since Simran told me you have gone on leave!' he growled on the phone.

'Wha . . .?' Janaki said drowsily.

'Are you drunk? I won't hold it against you if you are.'

'No yaar, don't have a drop of alcohol in the house. You're welcome to bring some over, though!' The idea of spending the evening alone was suddenly not so appealing. Kajal was out of town again, and Janaki felt like some company.

'Theek hai, have a bottle of Old Monk; lekar aata hoon. Sambar chawal toh khilaogi?'

'Sure,' she said, relieved to have some company after all.

Janaki checked her phone for other missed calls and messages. There were a couple of texts from Simran, a little worried at not having her calls answered. Janaki quickly responded, and stopped looking for the one call that might make all of this all right— Vishnu, calling to apologize.

She had all these fantasy scenarios where Vishnu would beg her to take him back, apologize profusely for ratting on her and ride off into the sunset, showering her with those improbable, delicious kisses. In every one of those fantasies she took him back. And that's why they are fantasies, she thought to herself. She knew as well as anyone that it would take her a while to forgive Vishnu, and an eternity for him to forgive her.

She had done her penance, by exposing Uday Pratap, and she was doing more of it by being in the doghouse at work. After this, no more; I'm done, she said to herself and felt at peace.

She dragged herself to the kitchen and started grating some coconut for the sambar.

~

It was 11.30 p.m. and, unusually for them, both Deepak and Janaki were piss drunk, or, as Janaki was beginning to say, pish drunk. A bottle of rum had been consumed as though it was going out of fashion and, after trashing every reporter and his or her sources, the two were feeling fairly pleased with themselves.

It was while cutting a wide swathe through a mountain of sambar–rice, that Deepak suddenly asked, 'Janaki, what happened with Vishnu? Just tell me, yaar, kaan kheench ke saamne rakh doonga.'

Janaki told her story yet again, including Vishnu's dismissive attitude towards her job. Deepak was silent for some time and then he said, 'Look, all these government types are like that, so you don't have to take offence. They don't get us; we don't get them. As for the other, as I said earlier, I'm surprised that he snitched on you.'

'Leave it, Deepak. Just tell me, what should I do for the next two weeks?' she asked, jumping up from the divan where she was sitting cross-legged.

'Kuch bhi! Take a trip you've always wanted to take!'

That set Janaki thinking: two weeks, just what can I do in that time?

Eighteen

Vishnu stared at his desktop in disbelief. There it was, in black and white, Uday Pratap's fall from grace, penned by the woman who had become an aching regret with him. He wasn't stupid, he knew an apology for what it was, and Janaki had spelt hers out in black and white and hung it out for all the world to see. My sweetheart, he thought to himself, I knew you were the one.

Vishnu felt like a heel for having disparaged her, and her job, when she had showed raw courage in not just warning him, but also acknowledging that she had been used, and then wreaking this vengeance.

And what have you done? Come back to Chennai with your tail between your legs, he thought. His return was greeted with sympathy and a surprising amount of tact from his colleagues. He was not the first bureaucrat whose central posting had been derailed by political uncertainties. He had landed up with the industries commissioner's job in Chennai, and all in all he had managed to survive 'Apex-gate' well enough.

Communications were still down between his mother and him, something he intended to keep that way till he felt less angry with the world. He had even left Ramadin behind in Delhi, wanting no more of his mother's interference—cutting free at last. Makes me sound like a chump, but what the heck! he told himself.

Vishnu had thought Chennai and settling back into the rhythm of his life here would dull the pain of breaking up with Janaki.

With Gayatri, after a while it had become a convenient solace to think of her, and a shield against his mother's more obvious methods at matchmaking. He was older now, and he found that this time round it was much harder to bear. He had saved Janaki's picture on his phone, and he found himself looking at her face, and those eyes, a million times a day. And just as many times he wondered whether he had wrecked the one relationship in his life which could have worked. When he looked back on those heady days in Delhi, he couldn't recall a single instance where he wished he were somewhere else.

Vishnu found himself daydreaming yet again: a scenario where all the misunderstanding had not happened, where he and Janaki would marry, have babies and do all sorts of wonderful things together. Building castles in the air, instead of factories on the ground, he told himself sternly as he snapped out of his reverie.

The story on Uday Pratap plagued him though—it was a message from Janaki. A message that she had put herself and her job on the line for him, an apology of monumental proportions, something only a truly honourable human being would do. C'mon you little shit, get a move on and call your woman. She's shown that she has the guts to put her cards on the table, what are you waiting for? an insistent voice in his head said. Vishnu was almost ashamed to admit to the fact that he still felt hesitant about calling Janaki. His bosses in Chennai and Delhi knew she had broken the story on Purushottamam, and the link would still bother him in the years to come. Bureaucracy and politics survived on tall memories and damaging dossiers.

He picked up his phone and dialled Deepak's number instead. 'Wha . . . who is this?' came a mumbled response from the other end.

'Er . . . Deepak? This is Vishnu, from Chennai.'

He could almost see Deepak sit up straight at the other end of the line. 'Vishnu. Hi, what's up, boss?' Deepak said in a faux casual tone.

'Kuch nahin, sab badhiya. I'm back in Chennai, you know that na?'

'Yeah, I heard,' Deepak replied. And kept silent. It was a silence that was designed to get the truth out of Vishnu, about the reason for his call.

'Deepak, how is Janaki? I saw the story on Uday Pratap this morning.'

'She's good. That came out yesterday here, they must have uploaded it a day later on the online edition,' he replied, pretending to be obtuse.

Vishnu sighed, and decided to take the plunge. 'Deepak, I need to know how she is.'

'Then why don't you frigging call her, man? You piled on to her when she went out of the way for you, dude, and you snitched about her to that bitch of a woman!' He was almost shouting at Vishnu.

Vishnu was a little taken aback at the turn the conversation had taken. For a minute he thought that Deepak was giving him a tough time over his disparaging remarks on being a journalist, but the second part of the sentence just didn't make sense.

'Wait a minute, just what the hell are you talking about?' Vishnu said, raising his voice as well. 'What the hell do you mean by my snitching out Janaki? And to which bitch!' he yelled back.

There was silence. After a while, Deepak replied. 'Oh, you're good. First you tell that bitch Shakira that Janaki warned you about the Apex story, and now you're pretending to be innocent. Just two people were privy to that conversation, you and Janaki—just how in the hell did Shakira find out unless you told her? Because the last time I checked, Janaki liked having a job and a good reputation with it!'

'Shakira? Man, I didn't even meet her after I came to Delhi except . . .' and then his voice tapered off. 'That bitch!' he yelled. 'Deepak, you've got to believe me, dude! I didn't tell anyone about this. But I do remember Shakira walking into my office the day I was packing up. She may have overheard my conversation with Ma; we were in a bit of a bust-up and I may have said something to Ma then.'

Deepak sighed. 'Whatever, dude. She knows and she came and told the editor here. Janaki was in heaps of trouble and had to submit a written apology. It took a lot of guts for her to do what she did Vishnu . . .'

'I wish I had known this was happening. You should have told me, Deepak.'

'Really?' Deepak replied sarcastically. 'You chump, didn't you realize what you had with her? She put herself on the line for you, and has done so again. That should have been enough. Get over yourself, Vishnu. You've gotten so used to playing it safe, I thought you of all people would realize what a gamble she took on you! Stop thinking like a babu and start thinking like a man!' he added for good measure, making Vishnu feel all the more ashamed of himself.

He knew, just as he had known when he was saying all those hurtful things to Janaki, that he was just being a crusty bureaucrat worried about his own job and career, which, at the end of the day, brought him very little joy and a questionable kind of solace.

'Do you have any idea where she is?' he asked Deepak.

'I was with her last night. After the story on Uday Pratap, she's been asked to lie low, so she's gone on leave for two weeks. She's tough; she's hanging in there.'

Vishnu frowned. 'Why has she been asked to go on leave? If the story is correct, then what is the problem?'

'Man, you are naive. Uday Pratap gave us the papers against Purushottamam. He is also facilitating some land for the paper's proposed hi-tech printing press. Do you get it now?'

Vishnu just shook his head in disbelief. 'Good god, that's just disgusting.'

'Oh yeah?' asked Deepak. 'How about when you turn a blind eye to what your political masters are doing, Vishnu? The important thing is that Janaki was caught in the middle of it and did her best to protect her integrity and yours, and you just launched into her.'

Vishnu sighed as he realized that Deepak was right. He had acted like a coward while Janaki had shown true courage. Hell, it took me a while to stand up to my mother as well, he thought to himself.

'Deepak, you're right, man. I shouldn't have left her like that. I'll call you again, let me call Janaki.'

As soon as he hung up he dialled Janaki's number, which was switched off. Like most people who set up house after the telecom revolution, she had no landline, only a mobile phone, which was supposed to be on all the time. Since she's on leave, I guess she's switched it off, Vishnu thought to himself.

It was annoying, but Vishnu was now quite determined to make up with Janaki. Talking to Deepak had made him realize what a shit he'd been, and just what he had passed over. He was rubbing his hands across his face, mulling his next move, when Gayatri called him.

'Hello?' he said, a little surprised. After the disastrous dinner with Janaki, Gayatri and he had barely spoken. She had come to the small farewell party organized by his batchmates in Delhi, but they hadn't really had time for a private conversation.

'Gayatri, I didn't expect to hear from you! All well?'

There was a pause at the other end and then she said, sobbing, 'Pramod hit me, and I don't know what to do. He tried to hit Amol too, but the nanny rushed him out of the room.'

'Good god! Get out of there, Gayatri, at once! I thought this was a no-brainer. You and Amol do not deserve this, and you have to protect your son! Just get the hell out; stay with my mother if necessary.'

'I can't do that, Vishnu; my parents would be horrified! And it's not just that; I'm Pramod's wife, what will people say?'

Vishnu saw red. 'Gayatri, I had never pegged you for a coward. If you can't do this for yourself, you have a duty to your son to protect him. What will people say? Did anyone care when Pramod was misbehaving?' he almost yelled at her. 'I can only help you if you want to help yourself, Gayatri. My house is open; go and stay with Ma till you figure stuff out, but you have to decide what to do,' he said, finally drawing the line he should have in Delhi.

He thought about all the quarrels he had had with Janaki over this, needlessly provoking her jealousy over a woman for whom he felt only desultory affection.

Gayatri sniffed and said, 'You don't have to yell, Vishnu.'

Vishnu bit back a harsh retort and said, 'Then don't talk like a battered woman. You have a career, an education and independence; if you behave like this, then what should other women with less means do?'

'Fine. Could you please ask Aunty to expect me and Amol?'

'Yeah, I'll do that.'

As for Janaki, Vishnu decided to book tickets to Delhi as early as possible and surprise her. She won't have anywhere to run, he thought to himself with a grin.

Nineteen

Janaki switched on her phone after sleeping the sleep of the dead for most of the morning. She and Deepak had gone on a bender after a really long time and her head was pounding as though a thousand hammers were being put to work. 'Never again,' she said, a litany she had repeated on similar occasions. Jyotsna had probably come and gone, thought Janaki, since no one had been awake or alive to open the door.

She dragged herself to the kitchen, the first order of business being to make herself some much-needed tea. As the tea leaves brewed, she looked at her phone, which she had put to charge. She saw missed calls from a strange number, but didn't bother to call back, and she also saw some calls from Deepak.

Hope he reached home fine, she thought to herself. 'Hi,' she said as Deepak answered the phone. 'Are you okay? I got some calls from your number.'

'Hi. No, no, I'm fine; the autowallah dropped me off fine. I called because Vishnu called me up. He saw your story today.'

'Oh, accha,' Janaki said, a little stunned. This was the last thing she had expected.

'Yeah, and the mystery of how Shakira got to know that you had warned Vishnu has also been solved.'

'How?' Janaki asked, curiosity pulsing through her now.

'He was having a fight with his mother over the phone about you when Shakira walked into his office and overheard. She put two and two together and came up with twenty-two.'

Janaki let out a sigh of relief, and the keening pain in her heart ever since she thought Vishnu had betrayed her, eased suddenly.

'Really? That explains it.' She also kicked herself for not trusting her own judgement of people. Vishnu was one of the good guys. How could she have forgotten that?

'How is he, Deepak?'

'He's fine; he's in Chennai. He asked about you. He didn't know you had been through all of this; he was rather remorseful. Hasn't he called you yet? He said he would.'

'Arrey, my battery ran out last night; abhi phone charger par rakha hai.'

'Woh kar dega phone. So what are your plans for this afternoon?'

'Kajal and I are going to indulge in some retail therapy and go to a spa,' she said, the chirp back in her voice. The world seemed suddenly right again. Janaki hung up the phone to shower and change; Kajal and she were doing the malls in south Delhi and then going for a chocolate massage each. That should put some pep back into me, she thought happily to herself.

Every minute or so she kept looking at her phone, expecting Vishnu's call, but the phone didn't ring. As Kajal called her from outside the society gate, to pick her up, Janaki was a little deflated. She hung on to hope though, that Vishnu would call her, and said as much to Kajal.

'Haan, he will. Guys never lie to each other,' said Kajal, putting a totally different spin on things. Janaki barely suppressed a grin at that. She was also getting a wee bit angry at Vishnu. It had taken her a lot of heartbreak and effort to not think about him every minute of the day, and now she was back to her anxious state, just as he had left her. Hope is always a dangerous thing, she thought to herself.

Tramping through some high-street clothes shops, Janaki picked up a few well-deserved treats, like a short black skirt she had always wanted, and a shimmery chiffon top to go with it.

The spa they were supposed to go to was inside the mall, and both Kajal and Janaki had opted for the same treatments. It took them less than twenty minutes to be slathered in chocolate. Feeling rather sinful, they talked in whispers and tried to catch some shut-eye. Their peace was not to last long.

'So you think Vishnu is going to come back soon?' Janaki heard a very familiar voice say.

'Yes Aunty, I called him in Chennai and he went ballistic over Pramod. He almost ordered me to leave him and stay with you, and told me he will be in Delhi to sort out matters very soon,' another familiar voice replied.

Indira Singh and Gayatri Dhar had just walked into the spa oblivious to a chocolate-covered Janaki!

Janaki met Kajal's stricken look with calm. She motioned Kajal to be silent.

'When I told him you had moved in he said he is rushing to Delhi. Beta, I am so happy. We had the most awful fight over that reporter girl. She would have made him an awful wife. Thank god he is over her. When I pointed out what she had done to his career he couldn't agree more.'

Janaki felt the prick of tears; they rolled silently down the sides of her face. Kajal held her hand and the two of them remained silent for the rest of the forty minutes that they had to stay there. Indira and Gayatri had moved to the pedicure section, having opted to have their massages later.

As Janaki and Kajal walked out of the spa together, Kajal turned to her and said, 'Sun, don't go by what these women say, okay? It could be just wishful thinking.'

'Kajal, he had time to call up Gayatri and move her out of her husband's house, and he couldn't make one phone call to me?' Janaki said, with irrefutable logic. Kajal just looked sadly at Janaki. 'You know what pisses me off the most? I was almost over him! Then this morning he raises my hopes and dashes them to the ground again. I'm sick of this shit!'

Kajal looked at her steadily and said, 'Chal, let's get out of town for a few days. The house in Nighlaat has not been opened up in a while. The mountain air will do you good.'

Janaki nodded. 'Yes, let's do that. Let's just sack out and to hell with men. They can screw themselves till the cows come home for all I care!' she said biting out the angry words.

Twenty

Vishnu disembarked from the Chennai–Delhi flight a couple of days later, feeling rather pleased with himself. Deepak had told him about his conversation with Janaki and he was sure he would be welcomed with open arms when he turned up at her doorstep. He could just imagine the scene. He would ring the bell, Janaki would open the door, and be surprised. He would sweep her up in his arms, beg her forgiveness and take her against the wall before heading out to the bedroom.

Maybe not against the wall, he revised his fantasy to more doable flourishes, maybe the drawing room rug. Whatever; he couldn't wait to get to her place. He wouldn't even go to his house first. Indira Singh and Gayatri Dhar awaited him there, and they were the last people he wanted to see.

It was, therefore, a huge surprise to him to see a big lock on Janaki's door when he arrived at her place. Mrs Mishra, Janaki's nosy neighbour, was chasing after her grandchild when she noticed Vishnu.

'Yes, may I help you?'

'Er, Janaki's not home?' he asked, now a little deflated.

'Who wants to know?' she said suspiciously.

'I'm a friend of hers from Chennai, Aunty.'

'Beta, there is a lock on her door. She hasn't informed me of her comings or goings,' she said with a sniff, as though that was a character flaw of Janaki's.

Vishnu was crestfallen and turned back with a heavy tread. Thank god he had asked for his own car to pick him up from the airport. He drove through heavy traffic to South Extension and the two women he least wanted to see today.

His mother fawned over him as usual while at the same time making it very clear that he had to work for her forgiveness. Gayatri hovered around him, clearly anxious to have a talk. As soon as he and Gayatri found themselves alone in the drawing room, she said, 'Vishnu, Pramod thinks that you and I are an item, and the whole batch knows that I'm staying at your place.'

'Have you managed to get a lawyer?' Vishnu asked in clipped tones.

'Er, not yet, I'm just getting myself together.'

'I've booked an appointment with Lila Mathew for you for tomorrow and have asked Sunrise Estates to look for a place for you to rent. They've told me they'll have something in a week or so. I've told them to look for something near Amol's school, so don't worry.'

Tears welled up in Gayatri's eyes. 'Vishnu, you want me to leave? Why did you ask me to move in then?'

Vishnu had known this was coming. He spoke in calm tones. 'Gayatri, please don't cry. I thought I had made it clear that this would be, at best, a temporary arrangement. You couldn't stay in Pramod's house after what happened. You appear to be more in charge of things now; it's time to take the next step and divorce him.'

'I don't want to live alone, Vishnu . . .' Gayatri said and looked at him expectantly.

Vishnu sighed. 'I'm sure you won't be alone long, Gayatri, and you have Amol with you.'

Gayatri shook her head. 'It was such a mistake not to marry you.'

'Gayatri, don't go down that road of regret. I have moved on. I love someone else, and I'm going to marry her. Don't make it impossible for you and me to be friends by revisiting the past,' he said, feeling very cruel, but light as well.

Gayatri nodded and, as Vishnu left the drawing room, he could hear her sobs. It cut him to the quick, but he had thrown his hat in the ring for Janaki, and he was firm on that. 'Now if only I knew where she was and what she was up to,' he said.

His repeated phone calls reached a phone that had been switched off. He decided that he would lay siege to Janaki's housing society if necessary, but he would get her.

~

Janaki, meanwhile, was enjoying the cold weather in Nighlaat, a few miles away from Nainital. Kajal's family had a quaint cottage there and, with their tons of books and the family dogs for company, some time away was very welcome.

Janaki thought over the events of the past year and, for the life of her, could not bring herself to hate Vishnu. 'I love him, Kajal, I miss that dimpled chin and roguish smile.'

Kajal sighed and said, 'Look, even if what these women said that day was true, you need to call Vishnu up and ask him what the situation is. Have a talk, and make sure that if it has to end it is done with a sense of closure; you shouldn't keep wondering all your life whether you let this one slip away without even trying.'

Janaki nodded. 'You are right, Kaj; let me get back to Delhi and then I'll call him. I also need a special project to keep my mind occupied—I think I'll gather the papers on the Apex scam. Do you think I should put together a quick book on how the story panned out?'

Kajal nodded. 'That's fine, but will you reveal that the papers were handed over to you by Uday Pratap?'

'I'll talk to the publisher and see. I'll call up Shumona at Imprint. You remember her? She was in school with us. Let me put together a proposal and see,' she said, a little cheered up. Heartbreak or no, Janaki was not willing to let her work slide. It was a large part of who she was and she was determined that she would get out of this blue funk the same way she always did, by distracting herself with work.

'Theek hai, first order of business when we get home is to call Shumona and get this baby on the road,' said Kajal. 'Now will you please set the table, I'm starving!'

Twenty-one

Vishnu felt like he was in a Kafka novel. He was sitting in Mrs Mishra's overdone drawing room sipping tea, with her overexcited grandson clambering over him—the boy would get a sound thrashing from him very soon if he wasn't careful. 'I believe the LTTE is recruiting child soldiers again,' he mumbled under his breath.

'What did you say, beta?' Mrs Mishra enquired.

'Nothing, Aunty. The tea is very good,' he said, cursing Janaki for all this. The fourth day that Vishnu arrived and rang Janaki's doorbell, Mrs Mishra couldn't contain her curiosity any longer. She invited Vishnu over and grilled him in a way which would have taught the country's premier spooks and spies a thing or two.

She had decided that he was far more eligible than vague Saurabh, and had already got him to attest a ton of educational certificates for her various relatives, since, as a gazetted officer, he was eligible to do so. She was quite happy that she was facilitating Janaki's marriage to such an eligible party.

'Beta, have a cookie,' she said. Vishnu watched desultorily as Pappu, the Mishras' grandson, crammed cookies in his mouth two at a time. 'No thanks, Aunty, I have juvenile diabetes.'

'Since when, beta? Then you must have children very quickly, you know,' she said, her enthusiasm flagging a little at this information. Vishnu smirked to himself, and thanked god for some small entertainment.

It was at this moment that he heard the now miraculous sound of a key being turned in a lock next door. He immediately stood up and almost ran and opened the Mishras front door, to find Janaki, balancing a bag and her mail, and opening her front door at the same time.

Vishnu turned around and thanked Mrs Mishra, and fairly ran the distance between the two doors. Janaki turned around at the noise and was rooted to the spot. 'Vishnu!' she said breathily, in tones quite unlike her usual firm voice. She noticed Mrs Mishra standing at her own doorway nodding approvingly at the scene. If Vishnu's appearance hadn't baffled her, Mrs Mishra's attitude certainly did, for she had viewed Saurabh's comings and goings to her flat as nothing less than Janaki running a soliciting racket.

Vishnu had a fairly hunted look on his face and, by the time he reached her, he had snatched her keys, opened the door and shoved her inside her flat.

'What . . .?' Janaki managed to bite out before her mouth was crushed in a deep kiss, all tongue and suppressed rage. It seemed to go on forever, before Vishnu allowed her to come up for air. 'Where have you been all this while? I have been coming here for the last five days to this awful lock. When we are married you will not have a key to the house, madam, that way, you will always be home before me!'

Janaki raised her eyebrows. 'Being a little presumptuous, aren't we?' she said, her composure back and, to be frank, a little anger making her way into her spine. She arched her back and said, 'And is this the household we are supposed to share, with Gayatri Dhar being a part of it?' she asked cockily.

Vishnu looked down at Janaki; they were still stuck in the hallway leading up to the drawing room. 'Oh, so you know.'

'Yes, unfortunately, I overheard a conversation between your mother and that woman, where they spoke of how she is now a part of your household. Last I heard, bigamy was still illegal for Hindus in this country.'

'She has moved out, Janaki. I offered her shelter with my

mother because her husband beat her and her son up, and she needed help.'

Janaki immediately felt guilty. 'Oh, poor thing. Will she be okay?' she asked, slightly concerned.

Vishnu smiled; Janaki's compassion was quite easily aroused. It heartened him.

'Yes, she's found a place and she has moved. I've got her the best divorce lawyer in town. But why are we discussing her, where the hell have you been all these days?' he asked in mocked anger.

'I was at Nighlaat. I waited for you to call me and then when I heard that conversation between your mother and Gayatri, I couldn't stay in town.'

'I called you that morning; your phone was switched off. Then I decided to just turn up and surprise you. Remind me never to do that again.' He laughed ruefully. 'And now I want an end to talk at least for some time,' he said, and proceeded to kiss her thoroughly. As his lips made their way down her neck and his hand made its way up beneath her T-shirt, he felt Janaki stiffen. The move, so unusual for her, jolted him. 'What's the matter, baby?'

'I haven't done my legs.'

'What? What does that mean?' he asked a little bemused at the turn of events.

'I mean, you turned up so suddenly I haven't had time to wax my legs,' she said looking up at him quite piteously.

'Will you just shut up!' he said, and resumed kissing her. He wanted to go over every inch of her body, so that she would never forget that he was the man she loved.

As he got her out of her clothes, he too had a confession to make. 'Er, I thought we could do it on the drawing room rug this time, but my back's going to go, I think,' he said. Janaki laughed and dragged him to the bedroom, which smelt a little musty as it had been shut for a week, but Vishnu didn't care.

He wanted to take his time over her, and take it slow, but as soon as he entered her, the incredible warmth just engulfed him. 'I'm very sorry, baby, but this is not going to last very long, I promise you the big O in the next round!' Janaki laughed. As long as they were together nothing mattered. She knew there would be many more times.

As their breathing came back to normal, Vishnu felt Janaki's warm hands stroking his back. He closed his eyes and wished that he could be with this woman his whole life. She was far from demure and certainly not coy, but she was honest and had integrity in all the things that mattered to him.

'Baby,' she said tentatively.

'Hmm,' he mumbled, still feeling ripples of that climax.

'I have a confession to make.'

Vishnu raised himself and looked at her. 'What? What is it?'

'I did kiss Uday Pratap once.'

Vishnu frowned and a queasy, sick feeling took hold of his stomach. 'When was this?'

'The day you saw us at the restaurant. I'm not offering any excuses but seeing you with Gayatri upset me.'

'Damn right you can't make excuses! This was a day after we made love for the first time. How could you do it?' he said, climbing off her.

Janaki looked back steadily at him. 'I told you why; and I am not saying anything else. My actions following this have been very clear on how important you are to me, to the point where I compromised my job.'

Vishnu was about to tell her to go hang her job, when he stopped himself. She had a point, even if he was boiling with rage at the thought of another man touching her.

He paused, took a deep breath. 'How am I supposed to trust you after this?'

'I trusted you when you had another woman, whom you say you've never gotten over, living in your house,' she said simply. 'Plus I wreaked revenge on him for the both of us, Vishnu, and I'm paying the price for it.'

Vishnu put his hands on his head and brooded in a corner of the bed. Then he jumped out of the bed suddenly and went to the kitchen to get some water.

There were now no secrets between them. The time had come to either commit to each other or bail out for good.

He came back with a bottle of water and offered her some. He touched the soft downy hair on her leg. 'You were worried about this,' he said and looked at her.

She smiled. 'Yup. I'm not a fashion plate, but I'm still a woman!'

'Janaki, we will move past this. I'll need some time, though.'

Janaki nodded, relieved that she had confessed, and now she felt as though a weight had been lifted off her.

'Would you mind if I went in and took a bath? I've just gotten in from a journey and need to wash the grime off.'

Vishnu nodded. 'Do you want any lunch?'

'Are you offering to cook?'

'Yup, Spanish omelette or Maggi, your two scintillating choices.'

Janaki smiled and opted for the eggs. As she soaped herself clean, she wondered just how to get through to Vishnu. He appeared normal, but was clearly struggling to accept certain things.

She came out towelling her hair to a dining table set with her best cutlery and a perfectly fluffy omelette melting on her plate. 'Wow,' she said and dug into the lunch.

'How is it?'

'Great,' she answered with her mouth full. Even as she ate, Janaki realized that they had to address the elephant in the room. Not just Uday Pratap, but also the fact that their professions were very different, although sometimes their worlds collided. Janaki wouldn't go to the extent of calling herself anti-establishment, but her job had a bit of a subversive element, although the last couple of months had made her realize that that subversion could be hired by vested interests. As a job it gave her more freedom than any other, so she had made her peace with it. She liked writing and, as Simran had said, 'For every story you do at the behest of the editor, you can do three you truly do believe in.' It was a bargain she understood and knew was better than most.

She still had to convince Vishnu that he would come first with her. Jobs come and go, but for the life of me I don't want to hurt

Vishnu, she said to herself. She had realized after her visit to her mother that she should have opted out of the Apex story voluntarily. She wasn't proud of the fact that she ended up being insincere to both poles in her life: her love and her job.

After they cleared the plates away, they settled down on her bed again and switched on the television, where, in what seemed like a cruel twist of fate, Uday Pratap's grim visage appeared. He had been stripped of his party post and had declared that as 'a loyal soldier of the NRP he would serve the party without any post'.

Janaki sneaked a look at Vishnu and was shocked to see him grinning at her. 'My god, when you get after someone, you really do a thorough job of it, don't you?'

Janaki smiled. 'I don't like being taken for a fool. Darling, when I told my mother all of this she told me that the reason I fucked up was that I was true to neither you nor my job. I was confused or tried to be too smart about things. As I pondered over it, I realized that she was right. In all the days that followed after we fell out, I prayed to god that if ever I got a chance to set things right, I would tell you that this would never happen again. And while we are ruled by the respective ethics of our professions and jobs, our first commitment would be to each other. I have your back Vishnu, whatever trouble you may be in. For me you will always be right and the world will be wrong. I hope you feel the same way,' she said, her heart in her eyes as she gazed up at him.

Vishnu was quite overcome. She had declared her love in such beautiful words, he didn't know what he would say, could say, to top that. 'Janaki, sweetheart, I promise you, it will be the same for me. All these months away from you I realized that we have a special connection,' he said, hopelessly recognizing that his words were quite inadequate compared to hers. 'This is unfair, words are your business, while I'm a pen-pushing office leech. I don't have anything more to say!' he said laughing in protest.

Janaki climbed on top of him and said, 'You are sure though? I'm not your typical bureaucratic wife; I don't do flower shows and I am fairly messy,' she said looking deep into his eyes. 'I don't want you to later want me to do what other people's wives do.'

'As long as you don't expect me to entertain your insufferable colleagues and listen to hyperbolic tales of how they almost brought the government down,' he said, swatting her bottom.

Janaki smiled. 'You have a deal, Mr Singh. One more thing,' she said with a frown.

'Yes?'

'I'm going wherever you are posted. There is no way in hell that I'll stay with your mother in Delhi while you are not there! That is an absolute deal breaker!'

Vishnu frowned a little. 'She's my mother, Janaki . . .'

'I know that, Vishnu, and I will respect her and treat her with deference. But you know how she feels about me. You will not abandon me to her like you did that evening over dinner! In time I will figure out a workable relationship with her, because neither of us are getting out of your life.'

Vishnu nodded, not fully convinced that he was in for peaceful times, and yet those long evenings in Chennai, literally pining away for Janaki, came back in a rush. 'All right, sweetheart, we'll sort this out as we go along. Er, the hairy legs were okay when I was not looking; you could have shaved in the shower,' he said suddenly trying to lighten the mood.

Janaki yelped and hit him with a pillow. 'You horrible man!' she said as he quite easily overpowered her in bed. Silence reigned for a time in the bedroom.

Twenty-two

Janaki and Vishnu were married in a quiet south Indian temple in Bangalore, a major triumph for Mythili Rao, who had determinedly gotten her way around Indira Singh.

'I believe that in north India, the baraat goes to the girl's house?' she had asked plainly. Indira could only nod, as her son had quite categorically told her that he had chosen who he wanted and the logistics of how the wedding was to take place was entirely up to the two matriarchs.

Therefore the compromise was that the wedding would be in Bangalore, and the reception in Delhi, where both sets of relatives could bless the couple

The last six months had been a mad rush for Janaki and Vishnu, and, as both saw that their implacable mothers had dug in for a fight over logistics, they had decided, in a strategic move, to threaten to have a court wedding unless differences were sorted out.

Janaki's relatives were apprehensive that she might be burnt for dowry, while Vishnu's relatives barely suppressed their horror at not receiving any.

Vishnu and Janaki had reached philosophical levels of detachment from the entire thing, and decided that as long as they got to marry each other they didn't care whether it was in Bangalore or Timbuktu.

Shortly after Vishnu and Janaki reconciled, she went back to work and received a surprise phone call from Uday Pratap. As the private number flashed on her phone, she debated whether she should take the call or not. 'Well, I haven't done anything to be ashamed of,' she said.

'Hello,' she said as she picked up the phone. 'I believe congratulations are in order,' said Uday Pratap from the other end of the line.

'For what, sir?' She knew being addressed as 'sir' would irk him.

'You've gotten engaged I believe, to your gentleman friend from Chennai.'

'Yes, I have,' replied Janaki, not knowing where this conversation was destined to go.

'Well, congratulations!'

'Thank you.'

'Does he know about us?' he asked her. Janaki sighed. What was it with these grown men that made it imperative for them to be memorable to every woman they touched.

'About the kiss? Sure, I told him.'

'And he accepted it?'

'Sir, it was one kiss, and, as I said, stop being a girl about it. It's over and done with,' she said callously; she was beginning to feel quite pissed off.

'Does he know what a cold person you are, how unwomanly?'

'Listen, just because you couldn't trap me doesn't mean you have the right to say anything. Let me point out that you used the troubled father routine to get to me; that wasn't very manly of you either.'

She knew she had scored a point when there was silence at the other end. 'Janaki, I did not use any routine; I was genuinely attracted to you. Yes, the decision to give you the story was cynical, but as the days went by I was drawn to you. That was not a lie.'

Janaki was not convinced but replied anyway. 'Sir, it's all right, you know and I know that you are in a profession that gives second and third chances, so I haven't done you any lasting damage. As for the attraction, I won't comment on that. As you know I'm engaged and, although Vishnu has been quite forbearing, I wouldn't presume on his tolerance for long. Let's just not talk to each other any more.'

'Fine. Let's not. Goodbye then.'

'Goodbye sir,' replied Janaki and let out a pent-up breath she hadn't even realized she was holding.

That was the end of that, she thought to herself. She called Vishnu and told him about the conversation and they both decided that she should start looking for a job in Chennai soon.

'It feels like the end of something, doesn't it? I'm glad he called, it was closure of some sort.'

Vishnu remained quiet and Janaki shut up after that. Uday Pratap would not be mentioned between them again, if she could help it.

~

The bride wore a maroon Kanchipuram sari with a mustard border, had flowers in her hair and looked radiant. The groom, in deference to his wife's family, wore a veshti and *mundaas*, traditional Kannadiga headgear. They went through the elaborate ritual peaceably but drew a line at extended celebrations.

A fairly large reception was held in Delhi and was attended, among other people, by Vishnu's entire batch. He was after all the last standing bachelor among them! Gayatri, who was in the process of a divorce, was the only exception. The happy couple flew off to Conoor for an abbreviated honeymoon.

Janaki had to start work at the *People's Daily* in Chennai as a special correspondent covering the state government, and she hadn't been given much time to settle into her new home before that.

Ramadin, after much debate, had been added to Vishnu and Janaki's household, since Janaki would not cook meat and Vishnu couldn't live without it.

Indira Singh elected to remain in Delhi; relations between her and her daughter-in-law were frosty at best, but could still be termed a 'work in progress'.

Janaki and Vishnu decided that their first meal in Chennai would be at the same restaurant where they'd had their first date. As they gazed at each other across the candlelit table they were swamped by nostalgia and a bit of fear as well.

'How easily could this have turned out to be our last date,' she said.

'After you kissed me, there was no way in hell I would have let you go,' said Vishnu linking his hands with hers.

Janaki smiled and said, 'How about we neck in the car again?' As usual, she did not have to wait for an answer.

Acknowledgements

I want to acknowledge Parsa Venkateshwar Rao Junior, who first encouraged me to send this book off to the publishers; my dear friend Madhavi Purohit who steered it to the right people; senior commissioning editor at Penguin Vaishali Mathur who shrugged good-naturedly through many cancelled meetings and erratic writing; and the cool shelter of the Indian Women's Press Corps where I took sanctuary through the worst of my writer's block.

Loads of thanks to Josy Joseph, one of India's best investigative journalists, for helping me out with technical details in the story.